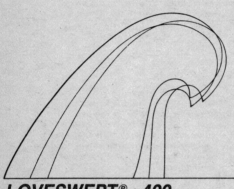

LOVESWEPT® • 400

Patt Bucheister
The Rogue

BANTAM BOOKS
NEW YORK • TORONTO • LONDON • SYDNEY • AUCKLAND

THE ROGUE

A Bantam Book / May 1990

*LOVESWEPT® and the wave device are registered
trademarks of Bantam Books, a division of
Bantam Doubleday Dell Publishing Group, Inc.
Registered in U.S. Patent
and Trademark Office and elsewhere.*

*If you would be interested in receiving protective vinyl
covers for your Loveswept books, please write to this address
for information:*

Loveswept
Bantam Books
P.O. Box 985
Hicksville, NY 11802

ISBN 0-553-44031-4

Published simultaneously in the United States and Canada

Bantam Books are published by Bantam Books, a division
of Bantam Doubleday Dell Publishing Group, Inc. Its trademark, consisting of the words "Bantam Books" and the
portrayal of a rooster, is Registered in U.S. Patent and
Trademark Office and in other countries. Marca Registrada.
Bantam Books, 666 Fifth Avenue, New York, New York 10103.

PRINTED IN THE UNITED STATES OF AMERICA

OPM   0   9   8   7   6   5   4   3   2   1

Meredith felt a tear escape the corner of her eye and trail down her cheek. Great, she thought wearily. She was about to break down and cry in Paul's apartment. . . .

She sank onto the sofa and buried her face in a throw pillow. When Paul came into the room a moment later, he thought she was sleeping. Then he heard her sniff and saw her raise her hand to wipe her eyes. Sitting down next to her, he lifted her onto his lap. "Go ahead and cry, green eyes. After a day like today, I don't know anyone who has a better right."

"I'm not crying." Her voice was muffled against his chest.

His hand smoothed over her back, soothing yet arousing for both of them. "There must be a leak in the roof then, because my shirt is wet."

She raised her head enough to look at his shirt. The blue fabric was completely dry. "Your shirt isn't wet," she said, glaring at him.

"And you aren't crying anymore," he said with satisfaction.

Before the sparks of temper could flare into full flame, he lowered his head and kissed her in the way he'd wanted to since the moment they'd met.

Passion overcame anger when he covered her lips with his. He had only to touch her and she came alive in a way she'd never thought possible. He threaded his fingers through her soft hair and rained kisses across her face.

"Meredith," he said on a breath. "If I don't stop soon, I won't be able to. . . ."

WHAT ARE *LOVESWEPT* ROMANCES?

They are stories of true romance and touching emotion. We believe those two very important ingredients are constants in our highly sensual and very believable stories in the *LOVESWEPT* line. Our goal is to give you, the reader, stories of consistently high quality that may sometimes make you laugh, sometimes make you cry, but are always fresh and creative and contain many delightful surprises within their pages.

Most romance fans read an enormous number of books. Those they truly love, they keep. Others may be traded with friends and soon forgotten. We hope that each *LOVESWEPT* romance will be a treasure—a "keeper." We will always try to publish

LOVE STORIES YOU'LL NEVER FORGET
BY AUTHORS YOU'LL ALWAYS REMEMBER

The Editors

One

"Is this an obscene phone call?" the woman asked, mildly curious.

"No," Paul Rouchett replied, startled by the unexpected question.

"Drat," the woman said in a disgusted voice. "This just isn't my day."

Paul choked back the urge to laugh. "You sound disappointed."

"It would have been the highlight of my morning."

He leaned back in his chair, cradling the phone on his shoulder. This call wasn't going quite the way he had expected, but it was a refreshing change from the others he had made during the past two hours.

"I could wing it," he drawled, "if it means that much to you."

There was a pause as though she were seriously considering his suggestion. Finally, she said wistfully, "Thanks anyway, but it wouldn't be the same."

"It wouldn't be that much of a hardship," he

said, propping his feet up on his desk. "You have a lovely, sultry voice. It wouldn't take much imagination for me to come up with some titillating suggestions."

"Well, thank you . . . I think." Her amusement was apparent in her voice. "I'll return the compliment, if that's what it was, and say that your voice is like warm whisky on a cold night. I didn't even think to reach for my whistle when I suspected you might be a pervert."

He found himself smiling, something he hadn't done much of the past seven days. This was a ridiculous conversation, but oddly refreshing.

"Thank you, I think," he murmured, repeating her earlier phrase.

He heard her chuckle, the husky sound vibrating through him like a warm electric current. His reaction to her voice surprised him. Maybe he should have listened to Tulip when she told him he was drinking too much coffee and not getting enough sleep. Then he wouldn't be fantasizing over an unknown woman's voice.

He shouldn't be wasting his time talking with her, either. When she first answered the phone, she had told him she wasn't the person he had called to speak to. He should be apologizing for bothering her, then hanging up so he could dial the next number in his accountant's Rolodex. She could be an eighty-year-old woman who just happened to have a sultry voice and an appealing sense of humor. Or a married woman with six kids and another on the way. Or a gorgeous blonde with warm green eyes.

He didn't hang up. "I'm sorry you're having a bad day."

"I didn't say I was having a bad day."

"Lady, if an indecent phone call would make your morning, I'd say today is not going to make the top ten of all-around-terrific entries in your diary."

A heartfelt sigh came over the line. "Actually, my diary would make pretty dull reading for longer than that. Never mind. I don't want to talk about it and you really wouldn't want to hear it."

He could sympathize. The past seven days hadn't been exactly a barrel of laughs for him, either. "Just out of curiosity, why did you think I was making an obscene phone call?"

"Wishful thinking perhaps. An obscene phone call would be a nice change from persistent salesmen trying to sell me vinyl siding, or anonymous wrong numbers."

He glanced at the small card he had taken out of the index. "All I did was ask to speak to Pinky. There's nothing obscene about that."

"You have a point," she conceded. "And I told you, there's no one named Pinky here. When you let your fingers do the walking, they must have stumbled over a couple of numbers."

Paul threw the card onto his desk to join the other discards. Another dead end. Still, grasping a weak straw, he asked, "How long have you had this phone number?"

"About a year."

That let out the theory that the woman named Pinky had recently moved and this woman had been given her number. He made one last-ditch attempt. "And you've never heard of a woman named Pinky Claryon or a man she knew, Dan Nichols?"

The woman's silence spoke louder than words. It was odd that he could sense her reaction even though he couldn't see her face and had never met her.

"Which name struck a nerve," he prodded. "Pinky or Dan Nichols?"

She still didn't respond. For someone who had been so chatty a minute earlier, the darn woman seemed to have turned downright shy. "Look, babe, I—"

"Meredith."

"What?"

"My name is Meredith," she said irritably. "Not lady or babe. It's fairly easy to say. Mer-e-dith."

Her astringent tone amused him. "Meredith what?"

There was another small pause, then she murmured, "Claryon."

At that moment, his office door opened slowly and a gray-haired woman stuck her head around it as though checking for uncaged lions before entering. When Paul slammed the palm of his hand down hard on his desk, the woman's head disappeared and the door was shut quickly.

"What the hell is going on?" he exploded into the phone. "I'm in no mood for games, Meredith or Pinky or whatever your name is. Why are you giving me the runaround?"

"You asked for someone named Pinky," she said, anger rising in her voice too. "You didn't mention the name Claryon. I am not now nor have ever been called Pinky. Nor do I ever want to be called Pinky."

He took a deep, steadying breath. Losing his temper hadn't accomplished a single thing over the last week, and it certainly wouldn't do any good now.

Drawing on the last of his patience, he said

quietly, "Meredith, I am trying to find Dan Nichols. Your phone number is in his Rolodex with the name Pinky Claryon next to it. If you can explain why your number and last name would be listed, I'd love to hear it."

There was only silence on the line. The thin rein Paul had on his temper frayed as the seconds ticked by. He was about to repeat his demand when she finally spoke.

"A man named Dan Nichols dated my sister when she was staying with me for a couple of weeks this month. He phoned Laura occasionally to arrange to see her, so apparently that's why he has my phone number. He picked her up here only once. The other times she met him elsewhere or at her own apartment. If he called her Pinky, it wasn't in front of me, so I don't know if she's the person you want."

Some of Paul's tension eased. It was ridiculous to be relieved that Meredith Claryon wasn't the woman involved with his crooked accountant. He didn't even know her. But that was how he felt. He shook his head in bemusement. There was no doubt about it. This fiasco with his accountant— his *ex*-accountant—was making him crazy.

He picked up a pencil and began to doodle on a yellow legal pad on his desk. "Where can I find your sister?"

"Believe me," she said, her voice tight with anger, "if I knew the answer to that, she wouldn't be called Pinky anymore. She would be called black and blue."

He knew the feeling. It was exactly the condition he wanted to leave Nichols in if he ever found the man.

"I'm sorry," she went on, "but I can't help you

locate Dan Nichols. I haven't seen or heard from my sister since she took off about a week ago. Considering she left with something that belongs to me, I don't expect to hear from her anytime soon."

Paul heard a muffled sound of pounding in the background, then Meredith said in a rush, "Someone's at the door. Since it will take me an hour or so to get there, I'd better leave now." She paused, then added seriously, "I hope you find Nichols."

The next sound Paul heard was a click as she hung up the phone. Frustration welled inside him as he tried to make sense of her statement. Either she lived in a large house or walked incredibly slowly, if it took her an hour to answer the door.

As he replaced the receiver, he glanced down at the pad in front of him. He had printed the name Meredith several times. Feeling foolish, he tore off the page and crumpled it up.

His door opened again. Looking up, he saw Tulip peek into his office once more.

"Come in, Tulip," he said, tossing the wad of paper in the waste basket. "I promise not to bite your head off."

The door was pushed open farther and a petite woman stepped into the room. The name on her paycheck was Gertrude Philippa Minor, but everyone called her Tulip. No one knew why; it was simply how she introduced herself. Her small stature and sweet, serene expression were deceptive. Though barely five feet tall and a skimpy hundred pounds, Tulip could hold a six-foot, two-hundred pound man at bay with only a look, or, if necessary, a lashing from her sharp tongue.

Tulip took care of the hiring, firing, and training of waitresses and bartenders at the Rogue's Den with a skill unmatched by anyone else in

Paul's employ. She was also the resident mother at the popular nightclub in Alexandria, Virginia, freely giving advice whether it was wanted or not. Perpetually wearing gray or lavender dresses with lace collars, she was like a character out of *Arsenic and Old Lace.*

She sat down in one of the chairs on the other side of his desk, making a clucking sound as she took in his rumpled shirt, two-day growth of beard, and red-rimmed eyes. "I guess I don't have to ask how it's going."

Leaning back in his chair, Paul shook his head. "I have one possible lead and it's thinner than the skin on an onion. All the other women I've talked to in the last couple of hours haven't seen Nichols in months, and they made it clear they don't want to, either. Except the last one." He jerked his head at the phone. "I just finished talking to a woman who's apparently the sister of his latest fling. The woman, Meredith Claryon, said Nichols called her apartment several times when her sister was staying with her."

Tulip frowned. "How is that supposed to be a lead?"

"Meredith seems a trifle miffed with her sister. I got the impression her sister stole something of hers and departed for parts unknown. She hasn't seen her sister in a week. Sound familiar?"

Tulip sat forward. "You think this woman's sister is with Nichols?"

He shrugged. "It's possible. I'm going to follow it up."

"Rogue, it took Nichols longer than a week to figure out how to embezzle your money. He's not going to make it easy for you to find him and get your money back. You hired him because he has a brilliant analytical mind, remember?"

Paul pushed his chair back, stretching his cramped muscles as he stood up. "Nichols isn't getting away with this, Tulip," he said, beginning to pace the floor. "Whatever I have to do to find him, I'll do it. I don't care how long it takes. I'm tired of people taking my money without doing anything to earn it. This is the third time it's happened, and that's three times too many."

Tulip's head swirled back and forth as he paced, as though she were watching a tennis match. "This is different from when you gave your ex-wives chunks of money to get rid of them. Nichols took the money."

Paul stopped in front of the large window of his office. The bright late August sun shone on the windows of the building across the street, and he half closed his eyes to shield them from the glare. He realized he hadn't stepped outside in three days.

His nightclub was located on the ground floor of the Lantis Hotel, but he preferred to keep his private office separate from it. Accordingly, he had converted five rooms on the twelfth floor into his living quarters. Tulip maintained an efficient office in the club, which the staff referred to as "command central." The assistant manager and bookkeeper shared the office, but no one was in doubt who was in charge. Tulip.

Before buying the hotel, Paul had lived in a converted warehouse just down the street. The purchase of that building several months before had required a great deal of his capital, and his accountant's embezzlement had set him back even further.

"I'll find him," he murmured, his voice like steel.

"In the meantime," Tulip said with customary

bluntness, "you have a nightclub where you should at least make an occasional appearance. You can't afford to alienate any of the clientele at this point, Rogue. This isn't a good time to lose business. Life goes on even for rogues."

She got up to open the door, and his assistant manager entered, carrying several tuxedos on hangers. Paul noticed the wary expression on Baxter's face. During the last week, his staff had been like a crowd waiting for fireworks to go off, hoping none of the rockets would be pointed in their direction. He couldn't really blame Baxter or any of the others. He hadn't exactly been all sweetness and light since his accountant had disappeared. Not that he had been either before the theft.

At least he now had a lead. A woman named Meredith.

A little after eight o'clock that evening, Paul returned to his apartment, going directly into his office. He yanked at his black bow tie to loosen it, then undid the top several buttons of his formal white shirt. The leather chair protested slightly when he sat down behind his desk. Leaning his head against the chair's high back, he closed his eyes and soaked up the silence. Usually he thrived on the energy and vitality of his club, but not that night.

He had caught the new singer's first show, shaken an assortment of hands, and suffered a dark scowl from Tulip when he told her he was going back to his apartment. The club had been unusually crowded for a Wednesday, but he would have preferred a quieter night. It was a poor attitude for the owner of a business that depended on the goodwill of its patrons, but the tensions and frustrations of the past week were catching up with him. All he wanted was a few minutes of peace and quiet.

So it was strange that he reached for the phone and stabbed out the number he had called earlier that day.

The phone rang twice before she answered. "Hello."

"Good evening, Meredith."

She was silent for a few seconds. "Ah, hi," she said at last. "I hate to disappoint you, but Pinky still isn't here."

It was there again, he mused, that odd soothing feeling of contentment just in hearing her voice. His response to her should have bothered him, yet it didn't.

"I didn't call to talk to your sister. I wanted to talk to you."

"Why?"

He smiled. "Talking to you this morning was the only good thing that happened to me all day. I decided I wanted to hear your voice again."

Meredith apparently couldn't think of a thing to say except "Oh."

"You're going to have to do better than that," he drawled, wondering abstractedly if he was losing his mind. "In case you're not aware of it, you need to talk into a telephone. Hand gestures and facial expressions are useless."

"I'm surprised, that's all. I didn't expect to hear from you again."

That made them even, he thought. He was a little surprised by his need to call her. "Did your day get any better?"

"It wasn't any worse," she said agreeably, apparently willing to humor him. "How about yours?"

"My day isn't even half over yet," he said, then he heard a strange plunking sound. "What's that?"

"My guitar." The amusement was back in her voice. "I was moving it off my lap and my hand brushed over the strings."

"Are you very good?"

She chuckled. "I'm real good at brushing my hand over the strings. It's when I try to play chords that I run into trouble."

He shook his head, wondering why he was grinning. "Do you usually play the guitar at eight o'clock at night?"

"The instruction book tells me where to put my fingers to create different chords. It doesn't say anything about a particular time I'm supposed to be doing it."

Her tart comments were only one of the things that appealed to him. He had always preferred tangy over sweet. He also couldn't resist a puzzle, and his unexpected reaction to this woman was definitely one he wanted to figure out.

Suddenly, there was a crashing sound in the background, then Meredith cried in alarm, "Ivan, no! Get away! Don't come near me."

Paul heard a muffled thudding noise, as though something or someone had fallen, followed by an exclamation of pain. He shouted her name into the phone but didn't get a response. Various strange scuffling noises came over the line, heightening his concern about what was going on. A loud clanging sound assaulted his ear as her phone apparently hit the floor. The line went dead.

Slamming down his phone, Paul quickly shuffled through the discarded Rolodex cards still on his desk until he found the one with her phone number and address on it.

The elevator was painfully slow as he descended to the ground floor. After quickly telling Tulip he was going out, he let nothing or no one get in his way as he strode out the back entrance of the hotel to where his car was parked.

He wasn't familiar with the part of Alexandria where Meredith lived, and it took him thirty minutes to find her. The address on the card was for an older two-story house set back from the road, and a notation on the card indicated she lived in an apartment on the second floor. The first floor of the house was dark, and there were no outside lights to help him see where he was going. He cursed under his breath when he stumbled into an overgrown bush partially blocking the walk that trailed around to the back of the house.

Stepping around the corner, he saw a sweep of wooden stairs along the outside of the house. Even though there was only a thin railing between him and a long drop to the concrete driveway below, he raced up the stairs two at a time. Shouting Meredith's name, he pounded on the door at the top. When he didn't get a response, he stepped back as far as the small landing would allow, raised his leg, and kicked the door.

His shoulder finished the job, and he shoved the door open. Rushing into the apartment, he stopped abruptly when he saw a dog, a very large black Labrador, standing directly in his path. The dog wasn't growling or baring his teeth, but his formidable size was enough to keep Paul from venturing any farther, just in case the dog decided to do either one or both.

"I didn't realize burglars ever dressed so well."

Paul tore his gaze away from the dog to the source of the familiar voice. He found himself looking into the most astonishingly brilliant green eyes he had ever seen.

"You'll find slim pickings here," she went on, her voice surprisingly calm. "I have exactly six dollars and fifty-two cents in my purse and a credit card over its limit."

Relief flooded through him when he saw she appeared to be all right. She was sitting in a chair about ten feet away, apparently unharmed. Except her right leg, which was propped on a footstool and encased in white fiberglass from her toes to her knee. Considering it had been only a half-hour since he had talked to her on the phone, the injury obviously wasn't a recent one.

He studied her, admiring the short, wavy dark brown hair that framed her attractive face. She was simply dressed in a white shirt and denim skirt. As his gaze slid over her, he realized she wasn't as calm as he'd first thought. Her right hand was clenched around a crutch resting on the floor beside her chair. Evidently, she was prepared to defend herself.

Looking closer, he glimpsed fear in the depths of her eyes, although she tried to hide it. The fact that she didn't want him to see she was afraid made him even more curious about her.

It occurred to Meredith she should be doing something constructive like shouting for help or trying to call the police. Yet although the man had broken into her apartment, she didn't think he was there to steal from her. She had distinctly heard him call her name before he had forced her door open, and she doubted that was standard procedure for burglars. And there was something about the direct look in his dark eyes that made her believe he wouldn't harm her.

She wasn't sure what she could do if she was wrong. The cast on her leg would hinder her from getting away from him in a hurry. Her dog was big and might look threatening, but his bark was definitely worse than his bite. Of course, she reasoned, her intruder didn't know that.

But intruder or not, she'd never had a man of such virile impact in her apartment before. In fact, there had never been a man like him anywhere in her life.

His features couldn't be classed as handsome in the classic Hollywood style. His long, sculptured nose had apparently met a fist or two in the past, and there was a small scar above one brow. Neither took anything away from his overall appearance; they only added to his masculine appeal. His eyes were the color of rich dark chocolate, their expression serious and concerned as he stared at her. His hair was nearly the same color as his eyes, and was thick and neatly trimmed. He was tall, his body lean and muscled. Some men appeared like cardboard cutouts in a tuxedo. This man wasn't one of them.

He glanced at her dog, then carefully stepped closer to her. "Are you all right, Meredith?"

"How do you know who I am?"

"Your voice," he said easily.

Her eye widened in surprise as she recognized his. "You're the man who's been calling about Pinky. How did you know where I live?"

"Your address was on the card belonging to Dan Nichols. He's very efficient, even in his private life." His gaze flicked to her right leg. "Since you couldn't possibly have gone to the hospital, been X-rayed, and had this cast put on in the last thirty minutes, this obviously isn't a result of whatever happened while we were talking on the phone. Did Ivan hurt you?" he asked abruptly.

She blinked. "No. Why do you think he would hurt me?"

"I heard you call out for him to get away from you. Then I heard a sound as though you had fallen. Since I don't see a man here, I gather you managed to get rid of him."

"He was wet."

It was his turn to look confused. "What?"

"Ivan is my dog." She gestured toward the black Labrador, who was now sitting on his haunches. "When he got back from his walk, he was all wet. He jumped on me and I ended up on the floor when I tried to push him away." Gesturing toward the cast, she added, "As you can see, I have a slight problem moving very quickly or gracefully."

His gaze never left her face. "I thought you were in some kind of danger. It never occurred to me that Ivan would be a dog."

"Actually his name is Ivanhoe, after the black knight."

Bending his long legs, he hunkered down beside the footstool and placed his hand on her leg, just above the cast. "What happened?"

Meredith gazed at his hand resting on her knee. He was a relative stranger, yet touched her as if he had the right. She frowned at the unusual sensation flowing through her at his touch. Heat tingled on her skin, leaving her flesh sensitized. Oddly enough, it felt natural for him to touch her. Maybe she had hit her head and didn't realize it, she mused. Maybe she was just imagining things.

She forced her mind back to his question. "I accidentally stepped in a hole four weeks ago and broke my ankle in two places." Glaring at the cast, she added, "This charming fiberglass addition to my wardrobe not only prevents me from driving a car, wearing my favorite pair of jeans, and walking my dog, it is also a definite drawback to going up and down those stairs outside."

For the first time since he had burst into the room, he smiled. "So this is why an obscene phone call would have made your day. You have a bad case of cabin fever."

"Something like that. Don't you think it's time to introduce yourself? I generally like to know the names of people who break down my door."

"Paul Rouchett," he replied, giving her his real name and not the one his friends and staff used. He didn't want to be the Rogue with her, although he hadn't the faintest idea why he felt the need to make that distinction.

He glanced at the dangling chain lock, then looked back at her. "You could use better locks."

"They were adequate before tonight," she said dryly.

His curiosity rose another notch. "You seem to be taking this very well."

"Which part? The bit about a complete stranger wearing a tuxedo barging into my apartment and breaking a perfectly good lock? Or the fact that you have your hand on my leg?"

"Most women would be screaming their heads off for either of those reasons."

"I'm not the screaming type," she said. Although, she added silently, she did wish he would remove his hand. Still, she made no effort to move it for him. "I wouldn't be very good at my job if I were."

Touching her hadn't been such a good idea after all, Paul realized. In fact, just being close to her was having an odd effect on him, as her scent drifted around him. Straightening, he stood in front of her chair and looked down at her. "What do you do?"

Now that his hand was gone, she wished he were still touching her. "I'm a registered nurse, trained in emergency room and critical care. The hospital prefers their staff to handle whatever happens without having screaming fits. I imagine the patients appreciate it too. Believe me, in an emergency room we see just about everything. I don't shock easily."

Having been in a few emergency rooms in his time, he found it difficult to believe this slender woman was one of the efficient staff who dealt with everything from gunshot wounds to drug overdoses to accidents of all kinds.

He looked at her, really looked at her, as if the answer to why he was attracted to her could be found in her features. She was not stunningly beautiful, although her smooth ivory-toned skin and soft mouth were immensely appealing. She wore her silky brown hair in a simple short style of gentle curls, its cut emphasizing her cheekbones and wide eyes. She wore little makeup if any. Since she was seated, he couldn't tell how tall she was, although he figured she was of average height.

He suddenly found himself wondering how well they would fit together, how her breasts would feel pressed against his chest, her hips nestled to his lower body.

Hell, he cursed silently, stunned by the strength of his desire. He didn't need this. It was crazy. No, he clarified. *He* was crazy. He had enough to deal with at the moment. He didn't want to be tied in knots by a woman.

Now that he knew she was all right, he decided it was time to leave before he touched her again. Then he noticed faint lines of strain around her mouth and the stiff way she was sitting. Her hand was absently stroking her right thigh as though to rub away some discomfort.

"You weren't hurt when the dog jumped on you?" he asked.

She saw where he was looking and removed her hand from her leg. "When I fell out of the chair, I jolted my ankle and bumped my knee on the floor. I might have a bruise on my knee, but that's all. I didn't do any serious damage."

He looked as if he didn't believe her. "Are you sure?"

"I'm a nurse, remember? I know these things."

As an ache in the back of his neck, caused by tension and lack of sleep, began throbbing, he realized he didn't want to leave just yet.

"Would it be possible to have a cup of coffee?"

She stared at him, her expression one of amused exasperation. "You were right up front when they handed out nerve, Mr. Rouchett."

"I just asked for a cup of coffee, not your hand in marriage," he said, a teasing smile shaping his mouth. "I'll even make it if you point me in the right direction."

Feeling as though she were on a runaway train without any chance of getting off, she indicated a doorway. "Through there."

He slipped off his tuxedo jacket and draped it over the back of the small couch. "Try not to break any more bones while I'm making the coffee," he said. Removing his cuff links and rolling up his sleeves, he strode from the room.

Meredith stared after him, then shifted her gaze

to her dog. "Am I hallucinating, or is that man a walking steamroller?"

As usual, the dog had no comment. Now that all the excitement was over, he plopped down and settled his thick head between his paws.

"You have the right attitude, Ivan. We might as well just wait to see what happens next. It's not that we have anything else to do anyway."

She picked up the guitar from the floor and began to practice the three chords she had learned so far. Occasionally, she heard the sound of a drawer closing and the clatter of dishes, but she stayed where she was. Sitting still, after all, was much less trouble than moving.

She scowled at the cast on her right leg. All she had done was step into a hole while jogging. So much for exercise being good for her. The moment she'd heard the bone snap, she'd known she was in trouble. She was still in trouble, only of a different kind. She had used up her two weeks of sick leave and week of vacation time. The cast was going to be on for at least another week. A week or so of physical therapy after that, then she could get back to work. Her savings account had never had a particularly healthy balance before the accident. It was certainly in worse shape now since her sister had cleaned it out. The next couple of weeks were going to be rough.

If anything good could be said to come out of her accident, it was that she had a better understanding of the adjustments patients had to make when they used crutches. It would have been a lot easier to get around if she had a walking cast. As a nurse, though, she knew a compound fracture had to have a cast from knee to toes. As a patient, she found it extremely inconvenient.

After five minutes went by and he still hadn't returned, Meredith's curiosity made her put down the guitar and reach for her crutches. Nudging the dog with the tip of one, she said, "Get out of the way, Ivan. I'm clumsy enough without having to step over you."

The dog obliged, moving several feet away before collapsing back down on the floor. Meredith adjusted the crutches under her arms and took a couple of steps. Paul suddenly appeared in the doorway only a few feet from her. Startled, she misplaced one of the crutches and started to stumble.

Moving quickly, he grabbed her upper arm, pulling her close to his side to brace her. He looked down at her, then, without warning, picked her up, letting the crutches fall to the floor.

"What are you doing?" she asked, automatically looping one arm around his neck. "I was managing just fine."

"So I noticed," he drawled as he carried her to the couch. "I especially like the way you tried to skip across the floor on one crutch."

"I should warn you," she said sweetly. "Nurses know the best places on the body to really hurt someone who's giving them a hard time."

Paul chuckled. "Thanks for telling me."

He set her down on the couch so her legs were stretched out across it. "I came to ask you if you take cream and sugar with your coffee."

"Neither."

He took a step away, then stopped. "Do you think there's the remotest chance you'll stay put until I get back with our coffee?"

She glanced at her crutches, lying halfway across the room. "Unless I crawl, there's no way I can go very far without my crutches."

"Good," he said over his shoulder as he headed back to the kitchen.

Less than a minute later he returned with a mug of steaming coffee in each hand. He set them down on the coffee table before gently moving her legs over so he could sit beside her. As he handed her a mug, he caught her studying him with a strange expression in her eyes. "Why are you looking at me as if you're wondering if I've poisoned your coffee?"

"Your reactions puzzle me. Do you usually go around breaking down strange women's doors, then serving them coffee? It seems like an odd hobby to me."

He smiled. "This is the first time."

"Would you care to tell me why you've honored me with this exceptional visit?"

He took a sip of coffee, then turned to face her. "I have a proposition for you."

Two

Meredith stared at him. Considering how dull her life had been lately, this was turning into quite an exceptional evening. Of course, there was still the chance she was hallucinating.

With her free hand she pinched her arm, then grimaced. "Ouch."

"Why did you pinch yourself?"

"To see if I'm awake or dreaming. I'm awake." She smiled. "My diary is going to have a pip of an entry tonight after all."

He was captivated by her glowing eyes. "It's not that kind of proposition."

She watched him as he drank more coffee, wondering why she was feeling disappointed. "What other kind is there?"

"Earlier, you mentioned your sister took something of yours and you haven't seen her for a week. I have reason to believe she's with my accountant, who disappeared about that time. The proposition I have is that we work together, using what we each know about our respective thieves, to try to locate them and get our property back."

To give herself time to think, Meredith lifted her mug and took a sip. She was pleasantly surprised to find the coffee delicious. In fact, it was better than her own.

Studying him covertly, she hoped she appeared as relaxed as he did. When she was on duty at the hospital, she was accustomed to touching people, being near them. It was as automatic as breathing, a natural part of her work. So it was odd that the weight of his hip against her leg affected her the way it did, quickening her heartbeat and creating startling sensual images in her mind. All he was doing was sitting next to her, and she was more aware of him than she'd ever been of any other man. There was nothing sexual or provocative in either his actions or his behavior, yet an embarrassing heat was flowing through her.

Telling herself to get her mind back on the conversation, she lowered her mug and met his gaze. "I don't know how much help I would be." She glared at her cast. "I can't drive with this ton of fiberglass on my leg, so I've only been able to phone some of Laura's friends. I haven't come up with a single clue to where she might be. I know she hasn't been going to work. Her roommate said she paid her share of the September rent, obviously with my money, packed a bag, and said she was going to take a vacation. She didn't say where."

"If you could get around, would there be places you would look for your sister?"

She considered his question for a minute. "There are a few clubs she liked to go to. She met Dan Nichols in one of them. Someplace called the Rogue's Gallery or something like that."

"Den."

"I thought you said his name was Dan?"

"It's the Rogue's Den, not Gallery."

He sounded miffed, she thought, puzzled. She wasn't an expert on nightclubs, yet apparently he was. "Obviously, you know the place. Did you try looking for him there?"

His mouth twisted in a slight smile. "That's the last place he would be."

The harshness in his voice was in marked contrast to his smile. Biting her bottom lip, she studied him, wondering why he sounded so angry. She was startled when he reached over and touched her mouth with his forefinger.

"Don't do that," he said roughly, his gaze on her mouth.

Surprise widened her eyes, and her lips parted slightly. He withdrew his hand, but his touch left a trace of heat. She stroked her lips with her tongue as though to wipe away the tingling impression. His gaze lowered again to her mouth, then rose to her eyes.

Awareness flashed between them like heat lightning, unexpected and electrifying. The air seemed to crackle with sudden tension.

She tore her gaze from his, unnerved by the sudden surge of heat. "You were saying something about the Rogue's Den," she managed to say. "Why would that be the last place Nichols would go?"

"Because he would lose his pretty capped teeth if he ever stepped into the place."

Meredith thought that was a bit strong. She glanced back at him. "And you would be the one responsible for him losing his teeth?"

A corner of his mouth lifted in a faint smile. "It would give me the greatest of pleasure."

"Have you contacted the police?"

"Not yet. It's personal. I might turn him over to the police when I find him. I've discussed the situation with a friend of mine who's a detective with the Alexandria police force, but it's not official. Yet. Did you report your sister's disappearance and theft?"

"No, it's a private matter. She's my sister no matter what she's done. If I do agree to help you find your accountant, I would want your promise not to involve Laura in any legal proceedings. She might be selfish and foolish, but she isn't a criminal."

"All I want is Nichols." He changed the subject. "What about your parents? Would your sister go to them?"

"Laura definitely wouldn't go home."

Paul was tempted to ask why, but the flat tone of Meredith's voice and the sadness he glimpsed in her eyes warned him not to. "Are there any other family members or friends she would go to if she were in trouble?" he asked instead.

"I've called everyone I could think of. No one has seen or heard from her."

Ivan drew her attention from Paul by standing up and lumbering over to the door. Lifting a front paw, the dog scratched at the door and looked back at Meredith. She groaned. Walking Ivan had become a major production since she had broken her ankle. Several times a day, a neighbor boy took him out, but once in a while the blasted dog decided he wanted to go for a late-night stroll. Traversing the stairs with crutches was tricky enough in the daylight. At night, it was like trying to navigate an obstacle course in the dark.

"Would you get my crutches for me, please? Ivan needs to go out."

Paul didn't move. "You aren't going to take that dog down those stairs."

Using the arm of the couch for leverage, she stood up. "Getting the dog down the stairs isn't the problem. Getting me down the stairs is the problem. He has four good legs while I, on the other hand, have only one that works right and two sticks."

He frowned at the dog. "Those stairs are a death-trap. I'll take your dog out. Where's his leash?"

"I'll do it," she said, hopping from the couch to the chair. "He's my dog."

Several long strides brought him over to her. Grabbing her upper arms, he half lifted her and plunked her down in the chair. "You've already had one fall today. What are you trying to do, go for the best two out of three?"

The decision as to who was going to walk the dog was taken out of their hands. Paul hadn't closed the door completely, and Ivan stuck his nose into the crack, pushing the door open enough to squeeze through. Then he disappeared.

Meredith called after him without any success. She started to stand, but was stopped when Paul forced her back into the chair.

"Stay here," he ordered. "I mean it. Don't try those stairs."

He was out the door before she could argue with him. If he had given her a chance, she would have reminded him that the dog didn't know him and he didn't have the leash.

Going after them wouldn't do much good, she mused, considering both the dog and Paul Rouchett could be blocks away already. She did the only thing she could do. She sat and waited.

Propping her foot up on the stool, she again

glared at the cast as though it were her enemy. One more week. Seven long days and that cast was going to be history. If she had to gnaw it off with her teeth.

It was ironic that since her accident she'd had the spare time she had wished for over the years, and she hated it. At first, she had enjoyed the novelty of the days stretching ahead of her with no demands, no work, no commitments. By the second week, the thrill had been definitely gone.

She had worked her way through her list of things to do when she had the time. She had read every book she had bought during the last several years. Every back issue of the *American Journal of Nursing* had been carefully perused. Even sleeping late in the morning wasn't such a luxury after the first few days. And she would give anything to be able to take a shower without a plastic bag wrapped around her leg.

Twenty minutes went by before she heard the familiar sound of Ivan's nails on the wooden steps. The dog came bounding into the living room, his tongue hanging out. This time he didn't jump up on her, but settled for a pat on his head. He sat down beside her chair and looked toward the door, and she held on to his collar for extra insurance.

After a moment she heard solid footsteps on the stairs. Paul's entrance was less enthusiastic than Ivan's. He leaned wearily against the door frame and glared at the dog. There was a splash of mud on one leg of his tuxedo pants, and his shoes weren't as polished as they had been when he left.

"I have a suggestion to make," he said, "regarding walking your dog."

"What's that?" she asked.

"Get five hundred feet of rope, tie it to the door-knob, and let him go."

"What a good idea." She patted Ivan, who continued to look at Paul.

He frowned at the dog. "Meredith, your dog is grinning at me."

"He's happy. There's nothing he likes better than a good fast run."

Paul shoved himself away from the door. "At least I accomplished something tonight. I made a dog happy. Why would you have such a large dog in such a small apartment?"

"He wasn't this big when I brought him home from a pet store." She saw his scowl deepen and added, "Before I broke my ankle, I took him out for long walks and he got plenty of exercise."

"Do you have a hammer and a screwdriver?"

It took a few seconds for her to catch up with the sudden shift in subject. "Why? Feel like making a doghouse?"

"I'm going to fix your door. Some idiot broke your lock."

She mentally threw up her hands in defeat. Some things weren't worth making a fuss about. After all, he had broken it in the first place. "There's a small toolbox under the sink."

It took only a couple of new screws to fix the chain lock, then Paul bent down to examine the bolt lock. Meredith tried not to notice how his slacks clung tightly to his hips and thighs. She heard several clicking noises as he worked the lock, then he turned his head to look at her.

"There's nothing wrong with this lock."

Which meant he would be leaving soon, she thought, then told herself it was ridiculous to feel sad about that. "You must be very clever with your hands."

Some emotion darkened his eyes as he straightened and placed his hands on his hips. "It was never broken because it hadn't been locked. That's not very smart."

"You mean a strange man could break down the door and enter my apartment?"

He couldn't hold on to his anger in the face of her amusement. "I suggest you make sure the door is locked from now on."

"Yes, sir."

He frowned at her, not certain if she was making fun of him or taking him seriously. Deciding he should leave before he did something crazy like touch her again, he carried the toolbox back into the kitchen. When he returned, he unrolled his sleeves, refastened his cuff links, and shrugged into his coat.

"If you hear from your sister," he said, withdrawing a slim wallet from the inside pocket of his coat, "will you give me a call?" He took a business card from the wallet and handed it to her.

She accepted the card without reading it. "You've never said why you want to find Dan Nichols, except that he took something that belonged to you."

He hesitated for a moment. He was not a man who talked about his problems easily, but under the circumstances Meredith had a right to know. More astonishing, though, was the realization that he wanted to tell her. "Dan Nichols was my accountant. He embezzled a considerable amount of money from my business." He tugged at the cuffs of his shirt until they were exactly the right length from the end of his coat sleeve. "How about your sister? Why do you want to find her?"

"Since I couldn't get around after I broke my ankle, Laura moved in here to help out. I gave her access to my savings account so she could transfer money into my checking account. She cleaned it out."

Watching her, Paul had the feeling there was more behind her simple statement than she was prepared to reveal at the time. "It looks like we have the same problem. Perhaps if we work together, we can find them and our money."

Meredith did want to find Laura, but if she spent much time with Paul Rouchett, she might discover more than she had set out to find. With her life so out of control, a man, particularly a man who was so attractive and intriguing, would be too much of a complication. "I'll think about it."

Paul knew that was his hint to leave. Considering he had broken the chain lock on her door and invaded her apartment, he had been let off fairly easy. At least she was considering his proposition and not turning him down flat.

"Would you bring me my crutches before you leave?" she asked. "I'd rather not have to spend the night in this chair."

Instead of doing as she asked, he picked her up. He ignored her cry of protest and carried her down the short hall to the only other room. The drapes were drawn over the single window, and the only light he had to go by was from the two lamps in the living room. He was able to see the outline of a bed in the diffused lighting, and he walked toward it.

Easing her onto the quilted bedspread, he lifted the cast and settled her leg on the bed. Her denim skirt was twisted under her, exposing part of her thigh. He didn't do a thing about straightening it.

He turned on the bedside lamp before leaving the room, then returned with her crutches. "Where do you want these?"

"On the floor next to the bed."

After he had laid them down, he remained beside the bed. "Can I get your nightgown or whatever you wear so you don't have to get up?"

"I can get ready for bed myself, thank you. All appearances to the contrary, I'm not an invalid."

He didn't know whether it was her pride talking or she was just cross with him for making her go to bed. He could understand both reasons. What he couldn't understand was why he was finding it so difficult to leave her.

Sitting down on the bed, he gave in to the need to touch her. He let the back of his forefinger trail over her jawline. "I know you said you weren't hurt when your dog jumped on you earlier, but you were shaken up. You should take it easy for the next couple of days."

"I'm sick of taking it easy," she said irritably. "That's all I've been doing for the last month." Taking a deep breath, she gripped his wrist and drew his hand down. "I'm sorry. You don't deserve that. It isn't your fault I'm not a very good patient. I should be thanking you instead of yelling at you."

He turned his hand and enfolded her fingers in his. "I would probably feel the same way if I were cooped-up for a long time against my will."

Her breath caught in her throat when he brought their clasped hands to his chest. She could feel his heartbeat accelerate against the back of her hand and knew her own was reacting the same way. Was she hallucinating?, she wondered again. That was as good an explanation as any why an attractive man dressed in a tuxedo was sitting on her bed holding her hand.

And why she wanted the hallucination to kiss her.

For a long moment, they simply looked at each other. Then Paul released her hand and rested his on the mattress, on the other side of her hips. Slowly, as though giving her time to stop him, he leaned down.

Shock vibrated through her as he covered her lips with his. There was nothing tentative about his claim on her mouth. As a nurse, she was aware of the reactions of the body to sexual stimulation. As a woman, she had never felt desire rise as strong and as quickly as with this man. He was virtually a stranger. Yet her response was as basic and elemental as breathing, stunning her with the exquisite pleasure flowing through her.

When he broke open her mouth and delved into the intimate warmth inside, she made a soft yearning sound. Her hands reached up to grasp his shoulders, to hold on to the source of the ecstasy, but Paul suddenly tore his mouth from hers and got off the bed.

Meredith dropped her arms. She couldn't read his expression as he gazed down at her. Nor could she understand why he had withdrawn from her so abruptly. If he was feeling only half the sensual awareness she was feeling, he would want more. The searing kiss had burned her to the bone, yet he didn't seem to have felt the heat.

"Meredith." His voice was slightly rough and husky. "This isn't what I meant to do when I came here tonight, but I won't apologize."

"I'm not asking you to," she said, propping herself up on her elbows.

Paul found himself wishing she would get mad as hell and tell him to leave. Maybe then he wouldn't be thinking about how good she tasted and how badly he wanted to touch her again.

"I meant what I said earlier, Meredith. I want your help finding your sister and Nichols."

Still breathless from the desire drumming in her veins, she wasn't interested in returning to their earlier conversation. But her pride made her treat the last few minutes as casually as he did.

"What makes you so sure they're together or will have the money? It's been a week since Laura disappeared. She could have blown every cent she took out of my account by now."

He clenched his jaw. "Whether I get the money or not, I want Nichols. No one takes something that belongs to me and gets away with it."

Meredith wondered if that applied to people as well as things. "All right. I don't know how much good I'll be, but I will try to help you find him."

He nodded abruptly, surprised at the strength of his relief. "I'll call you tomorrow." His gaze flicked to her cast. "If you start having any problems because of your fall, call me."

"My broken ankle isn't your fault. You don't need to feel responsible for me."

His eyes darkened with a storm of emotion. "Yes, I think I do."

With that cryptic statement, he turned and left her bedroom. She heard the faint click of the front door as he closed it after him. For a few minutes she remained on the bed, trying to make sense of the past hour. In such a short time, her life had been turned upside down and inside out by a man who just that morning had been only a voice on the telephone. Earlier, she had been com-

plaining to herself about being bored. That had
certainly changed!

Leaning over the side of the bed, she retrieved
the crutches and levered her heavy leg off the bed.
With her usual stumbling grace and lack of agil-
ity, she managed to get into the bathroom. While
she was brushing her teeth, she looked up at her
reflection in the mirror, then stared. Heated arousal
gleamed in the depths of her eyes.

"What is wrong with me?" she muttered, and
finished brushing her teeth. Before tonight, physical attraction had been only words. This was the
first time she had experienced the sensations that
were vibrating deep within her.

And the man responsible for those sensations
was a stranger.

Why had she responded to Paul Rouchett? He
was attractive, but she had met other handsome
men. Maybe the appeal was the bold expression in
his eyes, or the subtle sexuality in the way he
moved. Or maybe she'd been so bored the last
couple of weeks, she'd kiss any man.

It wasn't any of those things, she knew. Her
reaction to Paul Rouchett wasn't due to boredom.
It was him.

Even more puzzling than her physical response
was her emotional one. Once she had realized
who he was, she had felt unusually at ease with
him, as if she had known him for years. Instinct-
ively, she trusted him. Considering the blows people she cared for had dealt her in the past couple
of years, such trust was amazing.

And why, she wondered, had she let him take
over the way he had, carrying her around, making coffee, chasing after her dog? She wasn't used
to having someone run her life, even temporarily.

Ever since she had left her parents' farm in Nebraska for college, she had made her own decisions and taken care of herself, only rarely asking for help from anyone. Living at home had been suffocating, for her parents rarely socialized, and they and Laura and herself had forever been in one another's company. Once on her own, Meredith had clung to her independence with the tenacity of a vine grasping a brick wall. It was not something she would relinquish easily.

Before she went to bed, she hobbled into the living room and picked up the card Paul had given her. Expecting to see his name, she was surprised to see a drawing of a pirate and the name of the popular nightclub, The Rogue's Den. Now she understood why he had said Nichols wouldn't be at that particular club. Obviously, Paul had something to do with it. Considering he had been wearing a tuxedo, he could be the manager or perhaps even the owner. The card didn't provide that information, just giving the name of the club, the address, and the phone number.

She flipped the card over and saw another phone number with "the Rogue's private line" printed above. Odd, she thought. The first word wasn't capitalized. It gave her the impression the Rogue was a person rather than a place. Deciding it might just be a printing error, she laid the card back on the table. She would keep it, although she wasn't sure it would be a good idea to ever use it.

Returning to her bedroom, she removed her clothes and slipped a black satin nightgown over her head, enjoying the sensual feel of the cool material sliding over her hips.

Ivan ambled into the bedroom and walked in a

circle before settling onto the braided rug in front of a rocking chair in one corner of the room. Sighing heavily, he lowered his head between his paws and immediately fell asleep.

Meredith envied the dog. Sleep didn't come that easily for her after she slid between the sheets. She went over every word exchanged that night, every look, every brief touch. And the kiss.

It was easier to think of the proposition he had made than it was to relive the myriad feelings his kiss had loosed within her. She knew he wanted to use her to help him find his accountant. Maybe she should resent it, but she didn't. She wanted to locate her sister too. Perhaps they could use each other.

The motives didn't matter. She had agreed to help, and that was what she was going to do. At least she would be doing something constructive instead of sitting around doing nothing.

The prolonged inactivity had been driving her crazy. One reason she had chosen to work in an emergency room was because of the fast pace. She liked the feeling of being useful, of being needed. There was always something to do even on a relatively quiet day.

She might not have known Paul Rouchett very long, but one thing she did know, he would liven up her life.

Three

The following morning Meredith ate an apple along with her second cup of coffee as she stared at the stack of bills on her kitchen table. No matter how many times she looked at them or put them in different stacks or added up totals, she couldn't figure out how they were going to get paid until she went back to work. If her sister hadn't taken her savings, she could have hung on without much difficulty. There wouldn't have been much for extras, but she could have gotten by.

Gathering the various envelopes into one pile, she shoved them back into the kitchen drawer and slammed it shut. Whether she liked it or not, she was going to have to go to the bank and try to get a loan, or else sell the few good pieces of jewelry she owned. Her rent was due in three days, and she needed food.

If the situation between her and her parents had been different, she might have called them and asked for a loan to tide her over until she went back to work. But her father refused to speak to

her since she had left home, so she knew borrowing money was out of the question. Her mother
would never go against her husband's wishes,
especially in financial matters. Meredith heard from
her mother occasionally by phone and letters. Both
were unsatisfactory, but at least it was better than
no contact at all.

Stung by a sharp feeling of loss, she opened
another drawer and took out a small framed picture. The black and white photo was the only one
she had of her parents. Her father looked stiff and
uncomfortable in his Sunday suit; Alice Claryon's
smile was as faded as her best dress. The occasion
was Meredith's high school graduation, one of the
few times her parents had attended a school
function.

No matter how many years or miles separated
them, Meredith still felt a strong sadness. Neither
of her parents had approved of her leaving after
college to go far away to a big city rather than
moving back home. They didn't accept her argument that she could make more money and get
more experience in a larger hospital.

Meredith had no regrets about taking the offer
made by a nurse recruiter who had visited her
college. He had provided the ticket away from the
farm, and she had used it. Her father had called
her selfish. Perhaps she had been. She was also
more challenged and more contented than she
would have been living on the farm.

She had made mistakes in the past couple of
years. Getting involved with Eric Thomasville was
one of the bigger ones that came to mind. Like
her father, Eric had set ideas of how she should
live, and they weren't hers. She wasn't about to
make that mistake again.

Whether or not it would work, she was still planning to go home at Christmas to try to make peace with her parents. Being estranged from them was painful, and she hadn't given up trying to heal the breach between them. It had been two years since she had left Nebraska, two years since she had seen either of her parents, and she hoped it wouldn't be much longer than that. She didn't expect them to be happy about her being so far from home, but she hoped they would at least accept it and maybe eventually understand.

Having her sister also leave home to move to Alexandria didn't help the situation. For all Meredith knew, her parents believed she was responsible. It had been solely Laura's decision, though. Meredith hadn't even known Laura was coming until she had literally shown up on her doorstep.

Shaking off her dismal thoughts, Meredith stood up. As she left the kitchen, one of the crutches caught on a rug and she nearly tripped. Mumbling a few choice words under her breath, she righted herself. A few feet away from her chair, she stopped. She hated the thought of spending another day in that damn chair. She looked around the small living room. That didn't leave her with many choices. She had tried the couch and had found it inconvenient, since the telephone, books, guitar, and other things she used to amuse herself were by the chair. It would take a number of trips to move everything over. It wasn't worth it.

She could go downstairs and spend time with Mr. Bowers. Her landlord always welcomed her company and played a mean game of gin rummy.

Or, she thought as her gaze fell on two mugs still sitting on the coffee table, she could stand there and think about Paul Rouchett. Ever since she had awakened at dawn, his image had been almost constantly in her mind. She could still feel his hand on her leg, his strong arms as he carried her, his warm lips as he kissed her. And no matter how many times she told herself the entire evening had been an aberration, that if she ever saw the man again, an unsettling heat would not surge through her, she couldn't dampen her excitement at the thought that she might see him again.

Realizing she was standing there daydreaming, she pried her thoughts back to reality. She was too old to be acting like a teenager mooning over a boy. Which was exactly what she was doing.

There was a knock on her door, and she heard Billy Chommers call out. Ivan ran out of the bedroom and fidgeted while she fastened the leash onto his collar. Opening the door, she greeted Billy, then watched as Ivan practically pulled the boy down the stairs.

Thankfully, she had paid Billy in advance, so that was one less obligation she had to worry about.

She began pacing the floor, which wasn't easy since there wasn't much floor. When her hands became tired of gripping the crutches, she had to give in and sit down in the chair. Glancing at her watch, she saw it was only eight-fifteen. She groaned aloud and leaned her head back. Another long day spread out ahead of her, as empty of prospects as her bank account.

She jumped when the phone rang. Too out of sorts to talk to anyone, she stared at it as it rang two more times. On the fourth ring she gave in and reached for it.

Instead of her customary friendly greeting, she snapped, "What?"

"What took you so long to answer?" a male voice barked back.

"And good morning to you too, Mr. Rouchett."

There was a short pause, then he said softly, "Hello, Meredith. How are you?"

"Going out of my tiny little mind."

She heard his deep chuckle and felt a strange feathery sensation in her stomach. "We're going to fix that," he said. "Do you like Chinese food?"

When on a runaway roller coaster, she mused, there was no choice but to hang on tight and ride it out. "Yes, I like Chinese food. Do you have a particular reason for asking or are you taking a survey?"

"I have a particular reason for asking. Try to stay out of trouble. I'll see you later."

She was left hanging on to the phone with the sound of the dial tone in her ear. Shaking her head in exasperation, she replaced the receiver. Paul had an irritating knack for speaking cryptic lines, like an actor who had a few pages torn out of his script, leaving the main part of the scene dangling.

Still she had to admit she was no longer feeling as bored as she had been a few moments earlier. Since Paul had been vague, she was left wondering if he would call again or simply arrive on her doorstep with cartons of Chinese takeaway. Maybe he didn't plan to come over at all, but would just have some food delivered, out of charity.

During the rest of the morning and all afternoon, the phone remained annoyingly silent. The only person who knocked on her door was Billy. She tried to keep busy by reading and practicing a new chord on the guitar. She even turned on the television, only to push the off button on the remote control after the fifth commercial.

By six o'clock she had come to the brilliant conclusion that Paul had merely been making conversation. A strange conversation, at that, and brief.

For Ivan's last walk of the day, Billy took the dog for a long run while he collected for his paper route. When Ivan returned, he lapped up most of the water in his dish and sank wearily to the floor.

Meredith didn't have to worry about him making a dash for the door when someone knocked a few minutes later. She only had to worry about stepping around him. Leaning on one crutch, she opened the door.

The moment she saw him, she felt a quiver of reaction. Just the sight of Paul left her oddly breathless and grasping for reason. What was the matter with her, she wondered. She was a reasonably intelligent woman. She should know better than to be drooling over a man.

This time he wasn't wearing a tuxedo. He was resting one hand on the frame of the door, causing his tan raincoat to gape open. Underneath the coat she glimpsed a sparkling white shirt and dark brown slacks. Although it wasn't raining at the moment, there were dots of moisture on the shoulders of his coat and a few glistening drops in his dark hair.

"You'd better put on a raincoat or get an umbrella," he said.

She blinked. "Really? Why?"

"It's stopped for now, but it might rain again while we're out."

"Am I going somewhere?"

"You said you liked Chinese food. That's what we're going to have for dinner."

Since his hands were empty, she knew he wasn't

referring to takeout. She backed away from him, which was no mean trick on crutches. "I'm not going anywhere. I'm liable to hurt someone or knock over a table with these crutches."

Paul had expected her to refuse and had worked out what he would say to convince her to go with him. It had been difficult enough getting through the day without seeing her or talking to her, except for briefly in the morning. He was determined to spend the evening with her. "We need to talk about how we're going to find our two thieves. We can do that while we eat."

She wasn't ready to give in. "You could have a four-course meal in the time it would take me to get from the car to a table."

Instead of wasting time debating the issue, he stepped around her and opened the door of her hall closet. It took only a moment for him to find what he was looking for and remove it from its hanger. He held out a tan trench coat to her.

She made no move to put it on. "I don't want to go out," she said stubbornly. "It's more trouble than it's worth."

"I don't mind a little trouble," he said calmly, still holding the coat. "I'm here, aren't I?"

She tried another tactic. "I'm not dressed for going out to a restaurant."

His gaze took in her gray skirt and safari-style shirt, clenched at the waist with a narrow black belt. "You look fine."

It was not one of the most enthusiastic compliments she had ever received and didn't do much to change her mind. At least he wasn't as critical about her appearance as Eric had been. She supposed she should be thankful for that.

Meredith's lack of enthusiasm didn't bother Paul

in the least. He took one of her crutches from her and stuck her arm into a sleeve of her coat. To steady herself, she put her hand on his arm as he assisted her with the other sleeve.

"It looks like I'm going out for Chinese food," she muttered through tight lips.

He adjusted the collar of her coat. "Trust me. The worst that can happen is you might get a little wet."

His solution to her managing the stairs was to carry her down. Meredith didn't even try to talk him out of it since she doubted it would do any good. She wrapped her arm around his neck and went along for the ride. He carried her easily, but at the bottom he ran into his first obstacle.

Meredith's landlord suddenly strode around the corner, blocking their path. It was a toss-up as to who was more surprised, Mr. Bowers or Paul.

Mr. Bowers was the type of person polite society called "eccentric." He always wore bib overalls, a white dress shirt, and a striped railroad cap on his balding head. A retired insurance salesman, he immersed himself in model electric trains. Every room in his ground floor apartment had railroad tracks spread out on the floor, on platform tables, and on shelves along the walls. Vintage trains chugged through tunnels built into papier-maché mountains, on bridges over painted streams, and around small villages painstakingly constructed.

From his wide-eyed expression, Mr. Bowers was a trifle surprised to see his only tenant being carried off by a strange man.

"What's going on, Meredith? Are you being repossessed?"

"Not tonight, Mr. Bowers," she replied casually,

as though it were perfectly normal to be holding a conversation while a man was carrying her. "This is Mr. Rouchett, who's taking me out to dinner."

"Ah, I see. Well, I won't try to shake hands, Mr. Rouchett, since you seem to have yours full at the moment. I'm Jeremiah Bowers, by the way." He touched the bill of his cap and stepped around them. "You two youngsters have a good time."

Paul glanced down at Meredith after Mr. Bowers had disappeared around the corner of the house. "Is there a railroad around here I'm not aware of?"

Smiling, Meredith told him about her landlord's hobby. "Sometimes he lets the neighborhood children watch him put all the trains through their paces. Once in a while, their parents tag along. It's quite a sight when he has all of them going at once."

After he settled her in the front seat of his BMW, Paul returned to her apartment for her crutches. He placed them in the back, then slid onto the seat beside her. Before he started the car, he instructed, "Fasten your seat belt."

She struggled with it for a few seconds, but couldn't seem to get the latch into its proper slot. He leaned over to help her, and his fingers tangled with hers until the belt finally clicked into place.

While he fastened his own seat belt, she clenched her hands in her lap. Despite her lectures to herself all day, his touch still affected her, making her skin tingle and her heartbeat accelerate. She wanted to tell herself it was just her imagination, but she didn't really believe that.

Rain began to streak the windshield as they drove away from the curb, leaving trails of wavy

rivulets down the glass until Paul turned the wip-
ers on. Meredith didn't pay much attention to
where they were going until she noticed they were
driving down the main street of Old Town. She
didn't know of any Chinese restaurants in that
area, but apparently Paul did.

He stopped in front of the Lantis Hotel under a
covered canopy. She turned to ask him why they
were going to a hotel, but he had already gotten
out of the car. This time he didn't attempt to carry
her. He took out her crutches and assisted her
until she was standing on her own.

"I didn't know there was a Chinese restaurant
here," she said.

"There isn't."

Looking up, she was surprised to see the logo
for The Rogue's Den. The drawing of the pirate
with a black patch covering one eye and a red
kerchief tied around his head was rendered simply on a small sign over an outside entrance, separate from the hotel's main entrance.

"Are we going to The Rogue's Den?" she asked.

"No."

Meredith wondered why she bothered. She was
beginning to learn that Paul was going to tell her
only as much as he wanted her to know, and
nothing she said or asked was going to make any
difference.

A doorman in a gray and green uniform approached them. "I was wondering why you parked
in front instead of going around back," he said to
Paul. "Then I saw the lady on crutches." Turning to
her, he asked, "Is there anything I can do to help?"

She shook her head. "No, thanks. I can manage."

"Would you have one of the boys park the car in
my usual spot, Ralph?" Paul asked the doorman.

"Sure, Rogue. No problem."

Paul didn't look at Meredith to see her reaction to the name Ralph had used. Making explanations in public didn't appeal to him. He placed his hand at the small of her back to urge her into the hotel.

He stayed beside her as they walked toward the entrance, not trying to hurry her. He noticed that she seemed more embarrassed at her clumsy navigating than he was.

As he opened the door for her, he noticed a couple was about to exit at the same time. He stepped aside for them.

"Hey, Rogue," the man said when he saw Paul. "It's good to see you. We missed you the other night. Tulip said you had some important business to take care of." His gaze shifted to Meredith, taking in her crutches after examining her hips and the curves of her breasts with a look bordering on insolent. "I heard you were hard on the ladies, Rogue," he added, grinning broadly, "but not this hard."

Paul groaned inwardly. Of all the people they could have run into, it had to be Ross Steubbin. He was the type of man who emphasized every other innuendo with a sly wink and a nudge of his elbow.

Pressing his hand against Meredith's back to propel her through the doorway, Paul said, "Hi, Ross. Pamela. Excuse us. Meredith needs to get off her feet."

Ross poked an elbow into Paul's side, accompanying it with the inevitable wink. "Sure. I understand. As soon as we get home, I'm going to make sure Pamela gets off her feet too."

Pamela giggled as the door closed behind Meredith and Paul. Meredith sensed Paul's irritation as they crossed the lobby. He had dropped his hand, but she could feel tension emanating from him as he walked beside her.

"Charming man," she said lightly. "He reminds me of some of the specimens I've seen in Petri dishes in the lab."

The tension evaporated as Paul laughed. "I had a more graphic description in mind, but yours sounds better."

"Why did he and the doorman call you Rogue?"

Paul hesitated. He'd known the question was going to come sooner or later. Perhaps bringing her to the hotel hadn't been such a good idea after all. "It's a nickname I've had since I was a kid. It sort of stuck."

She looked up at him. "You're the rogue as in The Rogue's Den? The club is named after you?"

"It seemed like a good idea at the time."

"Should I be calling you Rogue too?"

"No," he said firmly, then surprised her by placing his hand at her waist again. "The floors are slippery here. You'd better watch where you're going."

In more ways than one, she thought, considering she was entering a hotel with a man called Rogue. She tried once more to find out where he was taking her for dinner. "Does your club serve Chinese food?"

"We aren't going to the club. We wouldn't have a chance to talk there. There would be too many interruptions."

When he stopped in front of a bank of elevators and punched the button to summon one, she decided it was time to reassert her independence.

"You're taking a lot for granted, aren't you? I'm not going to a hotel room with you."

He couldn't blame her for thinking the worst, especially after the remarks Ross Steubbin had made. He lifted his hand and briefly touched her cheek.

"Relax, Meredith. I live here. I'm not renting a room for a hot night between the sheets. I sent one of my staff to a Chinese restaurant for our dinner. It will be waiting for us in my apartment. If you feel uncomfortable coming upstairs with me, all you have to do is say so, and we'll go somewhere else. Or I can have one of the members of my staff have dinner with us."

He made her feel as if she were acting like a nervous virgin. "It's not that I'll be uncomfortable being alone with you, Paul. I just don't want you to get the wrong idea about why I'm with you in the first place."

The elevator door opened. Paul didn't move.

"I know why you're with me, Meredith." But he couldn't tell her why he wanted her to be with him. It was too soon. She knew one of the reasons, but not the main one. He changed tactics. "Unless you're afraid to be alone with me."

She directed her crutches into the elevator and hopped in after them. Turning awkwardly, she looked at him. "Our dinner is getting cold."

Paul smiled faintly. His instincts were right. She was a woman who couldn't refuse a challenge.

He stepped into the elevator and punched the button to take them to the top floor. When the elevator stopped, he held the doors open so she could navigate the crutches and herself into the carpeted hall. Then he led the way to his apartment, opened the doors, and waited for her to enter.

The crutches sank into the lush light gray carpet as she stepped from the tiled foyer into a spacious living room. A long maroon sofa and matching chairs were arranged in a grouping with glass end tables and a coffee table. The walls were a soft white, a neutral background for several large paintings.

Through an arched doorway Meredith saw a long mahogany table set with places for two. In the center of the table was a cut-glass vase containing three tiger lilies.

"Would you like something to drink?" Paul asked from behind her.

She glanced at him over her shoulder. "Nothing for me, but you go ahead if you want something."

He shook his head. "I don't drink."

He walked past her into the dining room and pulled out one of the chairs for her. As she carefully picked her way across the carpet, she mused over this new piece to add to the puzzle called the Rogue. He owned a nightclub that served liquor, but he didn't drink.

Like the living room, the dining room was quietly elegant. The crystal chandelier was opulent and reflected in the polished finish of the dining table. A low mahogany table stood against the wall opposite her, a painting hanging above it. She glanced at the painting and was unable to look away. She moved closer to study it.

There was something haunting yet magical about the seascape painted in soft shades of blue and gray. In the distance was a small island shrouded in mist. There was turbulence in the waves, counterbalanced by the serenity of the island.

She continued gazing at the painting, unaware of Paul watching her. He stamped down the urge to ask her what she thought of it. His artwork had always been for his own approval. He wasn't comfortable with the realization that he wanted hers too.

He didn't have to ask her opinion. She volunteered it. "It's like fantasy and reality combined. It's intense yet peaceful. It doesn't grab you by the throat like a sentimental memory, but grabs the heart, the inner soul, and hangs on."

Paul was stunned. She had described exactly the mood he had been trying to communicate when he had painted the scene. "If you'll be seated," he said stiffly, "I'll bring our dinner in."

Something in his voice made her turn her head to look at him. It was the first time in their brief acquaintance she had seen any sign of nerves in him. Surprise mixed with curiosity as she wondered what had caused his strange withdrawal.

She glanced back at the painting, then at him. "You painted this, didn't you?"

Very few people knew of his artistic bent, which was the way he wanted it. He shrugged. "Does it matter?"

Obviously, it did to him, Meredith realized, studying his closed expression. "It would matter if you ever stopped painting," she said sternly.

He relaxed, a corner of his mouth lifting slightly. Her spirited response wasn't the reaction he had thought he would want. He'd been wrong.

He gestured toward the chair. "Sit down," he ordered, adding, "Please."

Well, that was plain enough, she thought wryly. His artwork was apparently out of bounds as a topic of conversation. She hiked over to the chair he was still standing behind. After she was seated, he took her crutches and propped them against the wall behind her.

"Tulip was supposed to have everything ready in the kitchen," he said. "I'll go see what she's arranged for us."

He strode through the swinging door into the kitchen. Before it stopped swinging, he pushed it open again, carrying a laden tray.

After he'd arranged the dishes on the table, he returned to the kitchen. While he was gone Meredith glanced back at the painting. The man who painted that seascape hadn't just been playing with brushes and paints. She wasn't an expert by any means, but she could see and appreciate the sensitivity and artistic ability in each stroke, in the shading, and in the subject matter. This hadn't been painted by a womanizer named Rogue. It had been created by a man named Paul who had broken down her door when he thought she was in trouble.

After a third trip to the kitchen, Paul finally sat down. They both stared at all the food spread out on the table.

"Did you," Meredith asked with a bit of awe, "tell this Tulip person I hadn't eaten in over a year?"

Paul wondered what Meredith would think if he told her how surprised Tulip had been when he'd asked her to set up a dinner for two. His reputation was badly overstated. He rarely brought a woman to his apartment, and Tulip was aware of that.

He smiled faintly. "Tulip gets carried away sometimes."

"Tulip is an unusual name."

"She's an unusual woman."

"Does she work at the club?"

He chuckled. "She usually does as she pleases.

Is your foot bothering you? I could get a stool so you could prop it up."

She shook her head, more in exasperation than in response to his question. He was the most maddening man she had ever known. It was amazing how he could consistently dodge questions.

"No, it's fine," she said. "You've gone to a lot of trouble, or maybe I should say Tulip has." She paused while she considered whether or not she should ask something that wasn't really any of her business. She decided to chance it. "What exactly does a woman with the name of Tulip do?"

"Anything she wants to." He saw the flicker of irritation in her eyes and decided to clarify his answer a little more. "She's hard to describe. Think of General Patton, your favorite great-aunt, and a stevedore in a prim gray dress and lace collar. She takes care of the personnel, scheduling, hiring, firing, that sort of thing. Luckily, she's good at what she does. I wouldn't have the nerve to fire her. I like to keep my head."

"She sounds . . . interesting."

"She's that." He nodded toward the array of food. "If we know what's good for us, we'll make a dent in this."

She didn't need her arm twisted. She lifted the nearest bowl and ladled several spoonfuls of noodles onto her plate. "Do you think detectives usually eat this well while they're figuring out their strategy for solving a crime?"

"I wouldn't know. In movies, they usually drink beer and gulp down chili dogs, followed by antacid tablets."

She spooned out a generous helping of rice. "We might not be as experienced as they are, but we eat better." She selected an egg roll from the plate he held out to her. "So when do we start the planning session?"

"After we eat."

She knew she should simply enjoy the occasion and not question the reasons behind it. For the first time in what seemed like forever, she was out of her apartment, yet all she could do was question his motives.

"I hope you don't feel you need to entertain me like this while we're looking for the bad guys."

He leaned his forearms on the table. "One thing you should know about me, Meredith. I rarely do anything I don't want to do. You needed to get out, and I needed to be the one to take you out. It's not all that complicated."

She hesitated, wondering if she was going to make a giant fool of herself. "I think we need to get something straight, Paul. I don't want you to misunderstand why I agreed to help you. I want to find my sister to make sure she's all right and hasn't done anything really stupid. That's all I agreed to."

"What are you trying to tell me?"

She leaned back in her chair, certain now she was about to make a complete fool of herself. "Perhaps I'm presuming a great deal based on only one kiss, but I want to make it clear that I'm not interested in becoming involved with you on a personal level."

He didn't laugh or scoff as she expected. "It depends on what you mean by becoming involved. If you mean the happily-ever-after type of involvement, then I wholeheartedly agree."

Even though she should have been happy about that, Meredith's smile was slightly rueful. He didn't have to be quite so enthusiastic.

"I'm glad you feel the same way," she said with a touch of irony.

"I'm not in the market for a wife," he added. "I've had two, and I certainly don't want another one. But that doesn't mean I don't enjoy the company of a woman."

She wasn't sure whether it was the fact that he had been married twice that shocked her, or the casual way he mentioned it. He might have been discussing the weather.

As an experienced nurse, she'd believed there was little that could throw her off balance. She'd been wrong. If she was honest with herself, she would admit she'd been off balance ever since Paul Rouchett had appeared in her apartment. This latest tidbit he had tossed to her completely threw her.

Since he wasn't making a big deal out of it, she decided to do the same. She bit into the egg roll, aware he was watching her.

Hiding his smile, Paul followed her example and began to eat. He knew she had been startled at hearing he'd been married twice, but she wasn't about to comment on it.

During the long night and most of that day, he had thought about her without understanding why. There were the obvious reasons, of course. She was attractive, funny, and had a streak of independence that could irritate a man who didn't care for women who knew their own minds. He wasn't one of them.

The fact that he only had to look at her to want her didn't count. He had wanted to take other women to bed before. There was something else about Meredith. On the surface, she gave the impression of confidence and capability. Even when he had broken into her apartment, she had appeared cool and unruffled. It was the woman underneath he wanted to know.

Between the moo goo gai pan and the sweet and sour pork, they got around to discussing some of the ways they could try to find the thieves. Paul got a pad of paper and listed the people and places already checked out by either him or his detective friend, Michael Tray. Michael had not come up with anything so far either.

Finally Meredith stated the obvious. "We have a long list of what we've already done. What we need to do is think up some ideas for where we go from here."

Paul threw down the pencil. "There has to be something or someone we're missing. Some relative, some friend, something we've overlooked. But I'll be damned if I know what it is."

Meredith began to stack empty dishes and plates. "That's the conclusion I came to several days ago. I was hoping Laura would contact me."

"Leave those," he said sharply. "I didn't bring you here to do dishes."

The plates clattered as she let go of them. She slowly sat back in her chair and stared at him.

Paul's fury dissipated when he saw the expression on her face. Even though she tried to hide it, she looked as if she had just been slapped.

Four

Damn his temper, he cursed silently. "I'm sorry, Meredith. I didn't mean to snap at you. None of this is your fault, and I shouldn't be taking it out on you."

"You're right. You shouldn't," she replied bluntly. Although she didn't like bearing the brunt of it, she understood his anger. He was a man who, she guessed, hated feeling helpless, no matter what the situation. This was definitely a situation he couldn't control.

She reached over and picked up the pad of paper. "It doesn't look like we've accomplished much tonight."

"Last night you said something about your parents' home being the last place your sister would go, but you didn't say why."

She laid the pad back onto the table. "Our parents live on a farm in Nebraska near the South Dakota border. The farm is fairly remote, which is the way my parents prefer it. Working on the farm is their life. It isn't Laura's. She's extremely outgoing and social, and our parents aren't."

"Is that also why you left?"

"Partly," she admitted. "I wanted more than my parents had planned for me. Laura just wanted off the farm, but I had a desire to do something I couldn't do if I remained there."

"And that was nursing?"

She was tempted to tell him they were supposed to be talking about Laura, not herself. Yet she wondered if she revealed more about her own life, he might do the same. Whether or not learning more about Paul, and possibly being even more drawn to him, was a good idea was something she'd worry about later.

"When I was in the sixth grade," she said, "there was a grease fire in the cafeteria. The school nurse administered first aid to the two cooks who had been burned, managing to calm everyone else with amazingly soft command of the situation. Later that year, I got sick at school, and the nurse remained with me while I waited for my father to take me home. She patiently answered all my questions about nursing, telling me about her training and some of her experiences when she saw I was genuinely interested. Over the years, she encouraged me by lending me medical books and helping me get a scholarship to college."

"Alexandria is a long way from Nebraska. How did you end up here?"

"One of the recruiters who came to the nursing school my senior year was from Fairfax Hospital. I decided what he was offering was what I wanted. After I had found a place to live, Laura came here too. She stayed with me until she found a job and a roommate."

"How long—" he started to ask, but was interrupted by a sharp knock on the door. They heard it open and a man call out, "Rogue, are you here?"

"In here, Baxter."

Meredith thought Paul didn't look particularly pleased to see the tall, fair-haired man who appeared in the doorway. "I know you said you didn't want to be interrupted, Rogue," the man said, "but Tommy Peters is bothering Alicia again. You said to let you know the next time he comes around. Do you want me to call the police?"

"Has Tulip talked to him?"

The other man nodded. "He's had too much to drink. He didn't pay any attention to her."

"Then call the police. Ask for Tray. He'll handle it quietly."

"You got it." He nodded apologetically to Meredith. "Excuse me, ma'am."

Meredith smiled at the man. He left, and Paul pushed back his chair and stood up. "I'll drive you home."

"If you want to take care of the problem in the club, I don't mind taking a cab."

He brought her crutches to her. "I'll drive you home."

The touch of steel in his voice convinced her not to push it. She took the crutches without saying another word.

After they left his apartment, Paul was stopped several times before he finally managed to get her out of the hotel. Each time he was hailed by either a member of his staff or a customer he was polite but brief. Even when a strikingly beautiful woman in a slinky white dress clung to his arm and gushed over the wonderful new singing act.

By the time his car was brought to the front of

the hotel, Paul's jaw was tightly clenched. It had been a mistake to bring Meredith to his apartment, he thought. A major mistake. His original purpose for the evening was to get to know her better on his home turf. If they could have come up with ideas on how to find Nichols, it would have been an added bonus.

What he hadn't considered was the impressions she would be exposed to at the hotel. If he had made a list of all the people he wouldn't have wanted Meredith to meet, it would have contained every person they had run into.

The drive back to her apartment was accomplished in silence. Meredith didn't intrude on Paul's thoughts by trying to make conversation. She was too deeply involved with her own.

They might not have come up with any concrete plans for finding Nichols and Laura, but she had learned more about Paul. He was a man of varying moods, who lived well, if his car and apartment were any indication. The painting she had seen wasn't something she would have thought a man who had the reputation as a rogue would do. Her idea of a man who deserved to be called a rogue would own large nudes on black velvet, but not the sensitive scene she had seen in his dining room.

She thought about what the boisterous man had said when they had first entered the hotel. According to him, Paul had quite a reputation with women.

She glanced at his profile. It was easy to believe women found him attractive. Lord knows, she did. But he was more than a womanizer. He was a complex man, hard to read, maybe impossible to understand. And he'd been married twice.

She had been intrigued by the way he responded to the people who patronized his club, friendly but with that edge of distance. Then there were the few members of his staff she had seen. She could tell he was liked and respected, but he maintained a guarded remoteness even with them. And with her, she realized.

Perhaps if she hadn't seen the depth of feeling in his painting, she might have believed he was more the rogue others seemed to think he was.

Since he'd been burned twice on the matrimonial altar, she could understand why he protected himself from involvement. That was fine with her. It wasn't what she wanted either. She was more concerned with surviving than she was in entering into a romantic interlude. Maybe after she had her two feet solidly on the ground again, she could consider getting involved with a man.

Lately, she wished she could be more like Laura, able to shrug off any concern about such mundane things like rent or bills. Meredith had always been the practical one, the responsible one, while Laura concentrated on having a good time. Laura didn't stay awake nights worrying about money the way Meredith did. She let others do that.

Maybe Laura's way wasn't all that bad, she thought wearily. Having someone to lean on, to depend on, sounded very appealing at the moment.

Paul carried her and her crutches up the wooden stairs to her apartment, then used her key to unlock the door. Ivan barked excitedly when he heard the key in the lock, not stopping until Meredith spoke sharply to him after Paul opened the door.

She was about to step over the threshold, but

he put his hand on her arm. "Wait. I want to check your apartment."

She stared at him as he brushed by her. "What for?" When he didn't answer, she watched him go into the kitchen, then the bedroom. She waited until he returned to the living room before she asked, "What are you looking for?"

He checked the lock on the window as she entered the apartment, kicking the door closed with a crutch. "Humor me," he said. "I'm making sure everything is secure."

She tilted her head to one side as she studied him. "Paul, I happen to have a very big dog who wouldn't let anyone in while I'm gone."

The glance he gave Ivan was skeptical. "I broke down your door and he didn't do a damn thing. That's not much of a recommendation."

Satisfied all was as it should be, he walked past her to the door. He had his hand on the knob, had even turned it, but he changed his mind. Whirling around, he closed the distance between them in two long strides.

Standing inches away from her, he murmured softly, "Humor me."

His fingers threaded through her hair, holding her captive as he ran his lips over her jaw, leaving a trail of heat. A wave of desire washed over him. All the mistakes and blunders of the evening vanished when he covered her mouth with his. His fingers clenched in her hair, and he deepened the assault on her mouth.

Need clashed with desire as he absorbed the taste of her. She was more intoxicating than the finest wine, more exotic than a tropical sunset.

He was breathing heavily when he raised his head a fraction of an inch. He watched in fascination as she slowly lifted her long lashes to reveal her eyes glazed with desire. Her breathing was as labored as his. Experience told him he could have her if he persisted. Instinct told him it was too soon. He would win himself a night of release— and lose the small ground he had gained.

Taking a deep breath, he let his fingers run through her hair, finally releasing her while he still could. "I'd better go."

Unable to speak, Meredith could only nod.

He looked down at her for a long moment, waging a silent battle within himself. Sanity won. "I'll call you," he murmured huskily.

She watched as he turned and left her apartment. When she heard the click of the lock, she closed her eyes and pulled badly needed air into her lungs. She hadn't realized she'd been holding her breath.

Biting her lip, she tried to understand what had happened during the last few minutes. Her world had tilted alarmingly when his lips had claimed hers. It hadn't righted yet.

Shaking her head as if to clear it, she headed for her bedroom.

As she prepared for bed, she attempted to make a diagnosis from the symptoms she could recognize. Desire and passion had been only words before. Now they were real—and frightening.

The following morning she was awakened by a loud knocking on her door. Glancing quickly at her small clock, she saw she had overslept. She wrestled into her robe and grappled with her crutches before hurrying to the door. Ivan was sitting in front of it, his leash in his mouth.

Grinning, she bent down and clipped the leash

onto his collar. "Impatient this morning, aren't we."

She opened the door and handed the leash to Billy. After they left, she turned toward the kitchen. She needed a cup of coffee. Or a large dose of common sense. She had actually for one second thought it might be Paul knocking at her door.

As she passed the table her answering machine sat on, she saw the red light was blinking. The calls must have been made while she was out with Paul. She'd been so shaken by his kiss, she hadn't checked the machine before she went to bed.

Resting on her crutches, she pressed the play button.

The first message was from one of the nurses at the hospital who just wanted to say hello. The second message was from her sister.

"Merry, this is Laura. I just want you to know I'm all right." She stopped talking for a moment, and all Meredith could hear were strange sounds in the background. Then her sister continued. "It's not what you think, Merry. I need the money I took, but I want you to consider it a loan. I'll pay you back. I swear I will. Every penny."

Meredith rewound the tape and listened to her sister's message again. It wasn't the words she wanted to hear. Laura said basically the same thing every time she did something wrong. She was always sorry and promised to make it up to her. It was the noise in the background she wanted to identify. At first she thought it might be a radio, or possibly a television playing. She rewound it again. People were talking. A lot of people, which could mean Laura was at a party or a nightclub.

She stabbed the button to rewind it again. The music was different, not a band but a piano, and maybe a banjo. The faint crunching sound in the background didn't make sense, and didn't fit with the music and the cacophony of voices.

Frowning, she left the machine on record and hobbled into the kitchen. While she waited for the coffee to perk, she went over several possibilities that would explain the strange noises on the tape. Since her sister preferred a noisy nightclub to a quiet evening with a good book, it was easy enough to figure out Laura had phoned from one. The problem was the nightclub could be anywhere.

After pouring the coffee, she let it cool on the counter while she debated whether or not she should call Paul. There wasn't anything concrete to tell him, but she had promised to call him if she heard from her sister.

Be honest with yourself, she thought. She wanted to see Paul, wanted to hear his voice. Her sister's phone message was a good excuse. Of course, once she heard his voice she'd want to see him, and when she saw him she'd want to kiss him . . .

She used the time it took to drink her coffee to assure herself her wayward thoughts were under control and she could handle a simple conversation. Finally, she hitched up her crutches and made her way to her chair. She was anxious about her sister too. More often than not, Laura drove her crazy with her carefree attitude, but Laura had also been the first one on her doorstep after she broke her ankle. They might not have a lot in common, but they were sisters.

Paul's card was still where she had left it the night he had given it to her. Before she changed her mind, she dialed the number on the back of the card, the Rogue's private number.

It rang twice before a woman answered. Meredith's first impulse was to hang up without saying anything. She really didn't want to know that Paul was entertaining another woman in his apartment at eight o'clock in the morning.

She resisted the temptation to hang up and said, "I'd like to speak to Paul Rouchett, if he isn't busy. This is Meredith Claryon."

"Oh, hello," the other woman said in a friendly voice. "I hope you enjoyed the dinner last night. Baxter said you were as pretty as Rogue said you were. He's in the shower. Let me buzz him."

Meredith heard a throaty buzz, then Paul's voice and the unmistakable sound of running water. "This better be important, Tulip."

"It is to you, bub," she said tartly. "It's your lady."

There was a brief pause, when all Meredith could hear was the water. Then Paul said, "Hang up, Tulip."

The woman's chuckle faded as she did as he asked. Immediately after the click, Paul said, "Hello, Meredith."

Shock vibrated through her. All Tulip had said was, "It's your lady," and Paul had known it was her.

Now wasn't the time to think about what that meant. "You asked me to call if I heard from my sister. She called last night."

"Did she say where she was?"

"No. All she said was she was sorry she took the money, and she was all right."

"I suppose it's too much to ask that she would have volunteered her location."

The sound of water hadn't abated. She couldn't believe she was having a conversation with a man who was taking a shower. The water would be gliding over his tanned flesh, caressing his chest, sluicing over his hips . . .

She gulped in air. "There were some strange noises on the tape that could mean something if I could figure out what they are. I could be wrong, but I thought I heard a player piano and a banjo. Then there's an odd crunching noise fairly close to the phone." She paused, then added softly, "It could be someone cracking peanuts."

"Just a minute. Let me turn the water off."

It took only a second for the sound of the shower to stop. It was bad enough for her to visualize water running over his naked body. Now she imagined how he would look with his skin moist and gleaming.

"With the water running," he said, his voice clearer, "I thought I heard you say something about someone cracking peanuts."

"I did. That's what it sounds like. I've listened to it over and over, and it's the only thing it can be."

He didn't say anything for a few seconds. When he finally spoke, it was with disbelief. "A player piano, a banjo, and peanuts in the shell. Why am I having a difficult time figuring out where she could be with such marvelous clues to go by?"

Meredith sighed. "It could have been something on a radio or television, except there was also the sound of people in the background, as though she were in a rather large crowd. All we have to do is come up with a nightclub or a bar where there is a player piano, a banjo, and—"

"Peanuts," he finished for her. "Let me ask around, and I'll get back to you."

"Paul, Laura could have been calling from anywhere. She might not even have been in this state. I'm only telling you because I promised to let you know if I heard from her."

"It might turn out to be something." Suddenly he chuckled. "As much as I would like to continue talking to you, Meredith, I need to dry off and get dressed. I'll call as soon as I find out anything."

She was left holding a dead phone. Again. She could become, she thought, real irritated with his habit of ending phone conversations abruptly.

After Billy brought Ivan back, she fed the dog and went into her bedroom to get dressed. Her unmade bed was very tempting. It wasn't as though she had anything pressing to do for the rest of the morning. A couple of hours sleep might make her think clearer. Then again, maybe not.

She made the bed before she gave in to the desire to crawl back between the sheets. As she took out a white polo shirt and a short denim skirt to wear, the wish for a long shower came and went, as it always did each morning since her accident. When her cast was removed, the first thing she was going to do when she got home was to stand under the shower until the hot water ran out.

As she tugged the shirt over her head, she thought of the conversation she had just had with Paul. It would be fun to see Mr. Bowers's reaction if she asked the phone company to install a telephone in her shower. He would probably consider her request as strange as she thought it was that Paul had a phone in his shower. She couldn't imagine a call ever being so important that someone had to always have access to a phone, even in the bathroom.

Eric had prided himself on having the state of the art in every aspect of his life, but he didn't have a phone in his bathroom.

She struggled into the denim skirt, finally managing to fasten it at her waist. Checking her appearance in the full-length mirror, she remembered Eric's reaction when he saw this skirt. He had laughed and said she looked like a farmer's daughter. When she'd told him that's exactly what she was, he had stopped laughing.

Completely serious then, he had said, "All you have to do is burn that skirt and wear the type of clothing more suitable for your position as my date."

Even now, after a year, she found it hard to believe she had actually tried to dress to please him. She could admit she had been impressed with the limousines, the French restaurants, the concerts and theaters she'd attended with Eric. The naive girl from a small Nebraska farm had been overwhelmed by the big city life-style, wanting so badly to be a part of the fast lane, she had nearly bankrupt herself.

All she had to show for her relationship with Eric Thomasville was a closet full of expensive gowns she would probably never wear again. No, that wasn't all, she reminded herself. She had learned a valuable lesson as well. Never try to be anything or anyone other than herself. The benefits were self-respect. It certainly was a lot cheaper than trying to live above her means.

It was ironic, she mused, that when she had finally built-up her bank account again, her sister had depleted it.

Paybacks were hell.

From out of the hall closet in the living room she grabbed a jacket and Ivan's leash. The trip down the stairs almost became exactly that. She stumbled when Ivan galloped off the landing quicker than she planned to go. Luckily she managed to keep her balance. Maybe, she thought, it hadn't been such a good idea to wrap his leash around her hand.

When she was on solid ground finally, she knocked on Mr. Bowers's back door. From experience, she knew it might be a long wait. Just getting to the door over all the miniature train tracks was time-consuming. Assuming he heard the knock in the first place.

To her surprise, he opened the door almost immediately. "Hello, Meredith."

"Hi, Mr. Bowers. I was wondering if you happened to have a length of rope. I'd like to tie Ivan up outside so he can be out for a while."

"I think I have some around here someplace. Do you want to come in and help me look?"

She tried to get out of the invitation as delicately as she could. It wasn't only Ivan who would be hazardous to Mr. Bowers's trains. Stepping over and around the tracks was difficult enough with two good feet.

"I have Ivan with me, Mr. Bowers."

The elderly man had a solution. He disappeared briefly and came back with a large juicy bone. Ivan perked up at the sight of the tasty treat, wagging his tail and trying to jump up on Mr. Bowers to get the bone.

Smiling broadly, Mr. Bowers laid the bone down near the back door. "Tie the leash to the doorknob, Meredith. He'll be happy for a little while. I

THE ROGUE • 71

want to show you the waterfall I just finished. I had the darnedest time getting the water to recirculate. It was a real mess until I figured it out."

She smiled weakly and tied Ivan's leash to the doorknob as her landlord had suggested. There was no way she could get out of going into Mr. Bowers's world of miniature trains without hurting his feelings. All she could do was hope she didn't step on anything.

Paul didn't realize until he'd parked in front of Meredith's apartment that he was gripping the steering wheel so tightly, his knuckles were white. Dammit, he cursed silently. Where was she? He had phoned her three times during the last hour and had gotten her answering machine. Each time he heard her voice suggesting he leave a message, he became angrier.

And worried as hell.

His sense of responsibility for her didn't help take the edge off his temper. He found himself thinking about her at odd times, wondering if she was eating properly or getting enough sleep. Under the concern, he realized, was a sense of panic. For someone who spouted off about not wanting to become involved, he was showing dangerous signs of getting entangled in Meredith's life. Maybe he didn't want it, but he couldn't deny the possessive feeling was there.

He got out of his car and strode toward the house. Instead of going up to her apartment, he approached the front door. He was hoping her landlord might know where she was.

As he neared the door, he heard strange crunching and growling noises from the side of the house. Changing directions, he swept the large shrub aside and hurried around the corner of the house.

He stopped abruptly. Ivan was gnawing enthusiastically on something he held between his paws. Paul ventured closer, hoping whatever the dog was chewing on was something he should have.

The only acknowledgment Ivan made to Paul's presence was swishing his tail back and forth while he continued munching. Stepping over the dog, Paul saw the inner back door was open. He knocked sharply on the screen door. When there was no response, he knocked again, louder and longer. Finally, he heard a voice from inside yelling something about holding his horses. A few minutes later Mr. Bowers appeared on the other side of the screen, a puzzled look on his face until he recognized Paul.

"Mr. Rouchett, isn't it?" he said, smiling widely. "I'm generally not very good with names, but yours caught my fancy."

"I'm looking for Meredith, Mr. Bowers. Would you happen to know where she is?"

The bill of the railroad cap bounced up and down as Mr. Bowers nodded vigorously. "As a matter of fact, I do." He pushed open the door and gestured for Paul to enter. "Come in. She's in Talleyville."

If that was supposed to be helpful, it fell short of the mark. Reining in his impatience with difficulty, Paul asked, "How do I get to Talleyville?"

"Through Shady Grove, Coal City, and Bowers's Station. I'll show you."

Paul grabbed the door when it started to close as Mr. Bowers walked away. The older man's friendly voice became a little sharp when he realized Paul wasn't following him.

"Don't let the flies in, young man. One thing I can't abide is pesty insects."

Paul entered the house, figuring he was going to have to humor the man if he hoped to get any information out of him. He had taken only two steps when Mr. Bowers pointed a finger at his feet.

"Please watch where you're going, Mr. Rouchett. It gets a little tricky until you get out of Coal City."

Paul looked down. A set of miniature railroad tracks were laid out in a continuous trail a foot away from the door. Made-to-scale buildings and trees were arranged to represent a small village a little farther up the track from where he stood. He blinked several times, but they were still there.

In the distance he could hear the muted sound of a train tooting. Feeling as though he had walked into a fantasy world, he followed Mr. Bowers's example of stepping over and around the winding lengths of track. He crossed two other rooms carefully, one of them a small kitchen, complete with a train chugging happily along on a waist-high shelf that extended into the dining room.

The artistic side of him could appreciate the time and craftsmanship it had taken to create the miniature world inside Mr. Bowers's house. Perhaps at any other time he would have enjoyed examining the marvelous displays Mr. Bowers had painstakingly constructed. Right now he needed to find Meredith.

A small sign was tacked over a doorway leading into another room. It read TALLEYVILLE POPULATION: TWENTY-FOUR.

Mr. Bowers walked into the room and stopped. Over his shoulder Paul saw a large platform that filled most of the space. A train with ten cars hooked on behind the engine was buzzing around the tracks, which wound through a dwarf town. Little cars, trucks, and small people were set about in various places. Paul didn't take the time to count the people to see if there were twenty-four.

"Meredith," Mr. Bowers said, amusement in his voice, "your young man has come calling."

Paul stepped into the room and turned his head in the direction Mr. Bowers was looking. Meredith was perched on a high stool, her casted foot dangling in front of her. He saw the surprise in her eyes change to a mixture of excitement and desire.

His body stirred in response to the sight of her. Relief, arousal, and need fought for release and made his voice harsher than he intended. "Why didn't you call me to tell me where you were going? I've been going out of my mind worrying about you."

She blinked in astonishment, then stared at him. Neither of them noticed Mr. Bowers quietly leaving the room.

Meredith lifted her chin defiantly. "Who died and made you my keeper? I can leave my apartment without getting permission from you."

"You came down those damn stairs, didn't you?" he growled, striding over to her and gripping her upper arms. "You could have fallen and broken your neck, you little fool."

Pride stiffened her spine. "I am perfectly capable of taking care of myself. I might be a little handicapped at the moment, but that doesn't mean I've turned into a complete idiot."

"You could have fooled me."

As he gazed down at her, the flame of temper within him changed to fire of a different kind. Fierce desire tightened his fingers around her arm, and he moved closer until her thigh was between his legs. He saw heated arousal darken her eyes and felt a thrill of masculine satisfaction. She wanted him. Maybe as badly as he wanted her.

"Damn you," he muttered softly, then he claimed her lips.

His words had sounded more like a caress than a curse, and they vibrated through her as she responded fully to his kiss. She grasped his shirt as his arms slid around her, bringing her against him.

Time and place faded into nothing as they fed off each other. The clacking of the train's tiny wheels were a rhythmic backdrop for their accelerated heartbeats. Feelings that couldn't be said aloud were communicated by the murmur of a name, the intimate stroking of a tongue, the fevered touch of a warm hand.

Finally, reluctantly, Paul lifted his head. "You scared the hell out of me, lady." His voice was rough.

The fact that he'd been worried stunned her. "I'm sorry. I didn't realize you would object if I left my apartment."

He cupped her face, holding her gaze with his. "I'd object to finding you at the bottom of those damn stairs with your neck broken. If you want to go somewhere, all you have to do is call me and I'll take you."

Her heart thudded painfully as she absorbed his words and the meaning behind them. "It never occurred to me to call you."

Emotion flared in his eyes. "I realize that. And that isn't any easier to accept than the thought of your being hurt."

Meredith couldn't look away from his dark eyes,

wondering at the expression in them. Was it disappointment, or was it pain? Neither made any sense, considering he had told her he didn't want to become involved with her. Worry meant caring. Caring meant . . . what?

He dropped his hands and stepped back. "How long did you plan on staying here? I want to get to Springfield before two o'clock."

She shook her head, feeling as though she was dangling over a steep cliff. And her grip was slipping. "What's in Springfield?"

"Hopefully, Nichols and your sister."

Five

Meredith went to Springfield with Paul. Not because of the chance of finding her sister or because he'd taken it for granted she would go. She went because she wanted to be with him. If that made her as much of a mental case as he was for worrying about her, then so be it.

As he drove, Paul told her one of his staff knew of a small club in Springfield where there was a three-piece band consisting of a banjo, a honky-tonk piano, and a drummer. The patrons ate pizza, drank beer, sang along with the music, and munched on peanuts served in their shells. Everything fit with what Meredith had heard on her answering machine.

In an earlier phone call, the manager had informed Paul that the bartenders would be at the club at two o'clock. Even though it was highly unlikely any of them would remember Laura or Dan Nichols, Paul wanted to follow up the only lead they had.

An hour later they drove back to Meredith's

apartment. All the lead had provided was the certainty that Laura and Nichols had been at the club the previous night. One of the bartenders did remember them. So it was possible they were still in the area.

Before Paul turned onto the street Meredith lived on, they had to wait for a fire engine to dash across the intersection, its siren blaring. Finally able to turn the corner, Paul was the first to see the fire engine stop in front of Mr. Bowers's house. A few seconds later Meredith saw it.

"Oh, no! Mr. Bowers's house is on fire."

As Paul pulled to a stop they saw smoke billowing out of the front windows. The firemen had leapt off the truck, some unreeling the large hose while two rushed to the front door. Meredith had her hand on the latch of the car door, but Paul stopped her.

"You stay here."

"Paul," she said urgently, "Mr. Bowers could be in there. And Ivan is locked up in my apartment. We have to get them out."

"You aren't going anywhere. I'll make sure Ivan and Mr. Bowers are all right." He opened his door and started to get out, then spun back to face her. "Promise me you'll stay here, Meredith. With your foot in a cast, you can't move very well. I can't watch out for you and look for Mr. Bowers and your dog at the same time."

She hated it that he was right. She hated being helpless, dependent, unable to be of any use to herself or anyone else. She had to wait for Paul and the firemen to save Mr. Bowers and Ivan.

She looked anxiously toward the house. The firemen had disappeared through the front door, and the smoke seemed blacker and thicker as it continued to pour out the windows.

"All right, all right," she said. "I promise. Hurry!"

He didn't hear the last part of what she said because he had darted out of the car. As she saw his tall figure race toward the house, she added another name to the list of those to be concerned about. He ducked behind the bush at the side of the house, apparently intent on getting Ivan, knowing the firemen would help Mr. Bowers.

Neighbors streamed out of their homes, staring at the unusual activity. Several children had to be held back forcibly from running toward the house. Still staring at the back of the house where Paul had disappeared, Meredith jerked her head around when she heard the crowd cheer. Mr. Bowers was stepping off the porch, flanked by two firemen.

She couldn't stand just sitting there and doing nothing. Opening her door, she struggled out of the car. She started toward the house, but a fireman rushed over to her, refusing to let her go any farther.

Her gaze returned to the large bush shielding the side of the house. Now that she knew Mr. Bowers was all right, she concentrated on Paul and Ivan.

Its siren wailing, an ambulance skidded to a stop just beyond the house. The firemen escorted Mr. Bowers over to it, and he was given oxygen by one of the paramedics. Making her way awkwardly down the street, Meredith finally reached the ambulance. Mr. Bowers was sitting on a stretcher that had been removed from the ambulance.

"Are you all right, Mr. Bowers?"

He nodded, appearing strangely naked without his customary cap. Lowering the oxygen mask, he said, "The fireman thinks it's the wiring. The insulation is smoldering behind the walls in the dining room."

She made him replace the mask, adjusting the elastic strap around his head so it would stay in place. Even though the paramedic had already checked his vital signs, she felt for his pulse, automatically glancing at her watch to time it. She needed to do something, anything, to keep from rushing to see why Paul wasn't coming out of her apartment.

Satisfied with the elderly man's pulse and respiration, she saw the concern in his eyes and tried to reassure him. "The firemen seem to have everything under control, Mr. Bowers. Your trains are safe. Everything will need to be cleaned, but other than that, your trains won't be damaged."

Behind them, the crowd cheered again, and Meredith looked toward the house. Paul was striding across the lawn holding Ivan by the collar. There were black smudges on his face, his shirt, and his slacks. But he had never looked better to her. Ivan walked obediently beside him, apparently unharmed. It was doubtful her apartment had escaped the effects of the smoke, but thankfully Ivan had.

One of the firemen came up to Paul, and they talked briefly. The fireman gestured toward the ambulance, apparently in response to a question from Paul. He looked over, and despite the distance she felt the impact of his gaze when he saw her. He was furious. His anger could be caused by something the firemen had said, but she didn't think so. She hadn't stayed in the car as she had promised she would.

Still holding tightly to Ivan's collar, he strode toward her.

When he stopped in front of her, he gestured for her to take the dog. As she grasped Ivan's collar, he turned to Mr. Bowers.

"The ambulance is going to take you to the hospital, Mr. Bowers." Seeing fear cloud the older man's eyes, Paul placed his hand on his shoulder. "It's just to make sure you haven't inhaled too much smoke. A man named Baxter will meet you in the emergency room. Once the doctor releases you, he will bring you to the Lantis Hotel. You're going to stay there tonight. So is Meredith."

If he heard her shocked gasp, he ignored it. "Your electricity will be cut off until the firemen are sure the rest of your wiring is safe. If you need anything, ask Baxter, and he'll get it for you."

Resigned, Mr. Bowers nodded slowly. One of the paramedics assisted him into the back of the ambulance and the door was shut securely. As the ambulance started down the street, Meredith could see him sitting with his arms resting on his knees, his expression weary and sad. Her heart went out to the old man. The only consolation was that he hadn't been hurt in any way. At least not physically.

When she felt Paul move her hand away from Ivan's collar, she looked up at him. Still without speaking to her, he began walking toward his car, taking Ivan with him.

"Where are you taking Ivan?" she called after him.

He stopped and turned. At first she didn't think he was going to answer her. After a long tense silence, he finally said, "To the hotel."

"They won't let a dog in a hotel."

"Tulip is going to take him home with her," he said tightly. "She has a large fenced-in backyard. Do you mind if we continue this at the hotel? I'd like to get some of this smoke off me."

It was obvious he wasn't in the mood to debate the issue. She had second thoughts about defying him, but she had no choice. All the money she had was a little over six dollars, which wouldn't pay for a night in the hotel's broom closet.

"I'm not going to stay at the hotel." Her pride wouldn't allow her to tell him why.

He walked back to her. "Where else do you plan to stay?" His voice was quiet, too quiet. "In your car?"

"If I have to."

"You don't have to. Since you managed to get yourself out of the car by yourself, see how fast you can get yourself back in it." When she tilted her chin stubbornly, Paul's anger loosened its hold on him. There was enough of it left for him to threaten her, though. "I'll carry you if I have to. It might be a bit tricky considering I'm holding your dog. I can always let him go in order to pick you up. Of course, it might take a while to find him again, but . . ."

"All right," she said angrily. "You've made your point."

"It's about damn time," he muttered.

"I don't see why you're so angry. It's not my fault there was a fire in the house. You act as though it were."

He cupped the back of her neck with his free hand. "You promised to stay in the car and you didn't. I've had my fill of women breaking their word to me to last a lifetime."

"I was concerned about Mr. Bowers when they brought him out of the house. I had to make sure he was all right." She glared at him. "And I was worried about you too. At least by seeing if Mr. Bowers was all right, I was doing something instead of going stark raving bonkers wondering what was happening to you."

He eased his grip on her. "You were worried about me?" he asked, something close to awe in his voice.

The truth was so much more difficult to say than a lie. "Yes."

The tight line of his mouth relaxed as he smiled faintly. "I'll be damned."

She looked away, afraid she had already exposed more than she should. Some of the firemen were rewinding the hose while others were still in the house. It should be safe enough to go to her apartment now, she thought, and turned toward the house.

"Meredith, where in hell do you think you're going?"

"To get some of my things."

He stepped in front of her, blocking her way. "Your apartment is filled with smoke. Everything in it will need to be cleaned before you can wear it."

Stunned by the extent of the damage the electrical fire had caused, she stared at him, eyes filled with pain. She knew she should be thankful the whole house hadn't gone up in flames, but right then it was small comfort to her.

Paul wanted to take her in his arms and comfort her until the lost expression left her eyes. He didn't dare, though. He might never let her go.

He stayed beside her as she awkwardly turned around and made her way to the car. When he had seen the state her apartment was in, he had made a quick phone call to Tulip. The smell of smoke permeated every room although there was no actual damage. The arrangements he had made were for Meredith's own good—and his. There was no way he would be able to stand having her stay in a place that smelled of smoke, with soot coating every surface. She would thank him when she had time to think about what he was saving her from.

Catching her tense expression, he realized he might have to wait a long time for the thank-you.

After stuffing the dog into the backseat and making sure Meredith's seat belt was fastened, he maneuvered the car around the fire engine and drove to the hotel. When they arrived, the bell captain took Ivan to the baggage room, where he would stay until Tulip could take him home with her.

Tulip met them in the lobby. After introducing the two women, Paul took Meredith directly upstairs to his apartment. Tulip had been about to come with them, but he had shaken his head. Tulip had smiled broadly, not at all offended.

Meredith was too quiet. He knew she was shaken and distressed by the fire. On top of her broken ankle and her sister's theft, having a smoke-filled apartment was bound to be the last straw. She was one of the strongest women he had ever met, but at the moment she needed someone to lean on. And he was going to be that someone.

As they entered his apartment, he noticed how wearily she was handling her crutches. She was tired but wouldn't admit it. He closed the door solidly behind them, then put his hand on her shoulder. Prying one of her hands off the handrests, he saw how red and sore her palm looked.

In an instant he slipped his arm under her knees and lifted her. There was no protest this time. Her arm encircled his neck and she buried her face against it. His arms tightened around her. If it was up to him, he would carry her into his bedroom and neither one of them would leave for at least a week. But she had enough on her plate without adding a love affair when she wasn't ready.

He set her down on the couch, then knelt beside her, his hand on her thigh. "Are you all right?"

She missed his arms around her, but didn't feel she could ask him to hold her. "I'm fine."

And it would snow in August, he thought wryly, noting the strain in her eyes. Taking one of her hands, he rubbed the palm gently with his thumb. "You've been on those crutches too much today. Why don't you rest for a while? I'm going to call down for room service to bring us something to eat. Is there anything particular you would like?"

She shook her head. "I'm not hungry."

With some effort, he refrained from taking her in his arms. She looked so defeated, it tore at him. He had already pushed her further than she was ready to go, so he backed off. For the moment.

"I'm going to make a few calls," he said, "then take a shower and change clothes."

She nodded, hoping one of the phone calls would be to arrange for a room for her. She had a great deal to think about, and it was impossible to think clearly when Paul was so near to her. It was sinking in how close both she and Mr. Bowers had come to losing everything they had. She needed some time alone to think of what she was going to do.

Paul straightened and reluctantly left her on the couch. He purposely left the crutches by the door so she wouldn't be able to get up while he was out of the room. She would have to rest whether she wanted to or not.

After he left, Meredith leaned back and closed her eyes. In such a short time there had been too many drastic changes in her life. She felt as though she were being swept away by a strong current, out of control and without a life preserver.

She didn't know which would make her feel better, throwing something or having a darn good cry. Her mouth twisted ruefully as she decided if she didn't have bad luck, she wouldn't have any luck at all. Just that morning she'd been worrying how she was going to pay Mr. Bowers the rent on her apartment. Now she didn't have an apartment. At least not until it was cleaned and was habitable again.

Scrubbing the walls and floors with a cast on her leg was going to be a real treat, and it might take the rest of her life. What she needed was to approach each of her problems objectively. Doctors made a diagnosis and treated a disease after the symptoms had been systematically analyzed. Of course, hers might be terminal.

When she had broken her ankle, she hadn't shed a tear. It had been only a minor setback. She hadn't even cried when her sister had taken her money. Now she didn't have a bed to sleep in. Three strikes and she was out of the game.

A tear escaped the corner of her eye and trailed down her cheek. Oh, great, she thought wearily. She was going to cry right there in Paul's apartment.

She slid down sideways and buried her face in a throw pillow.

Fifteen minutes later Paul came out of his bedroom, tucking the tail of a clean shirt into the waistband of his tan slacks. His gaze was drawn to the couch. Meredith was stretched out on her side, her face hidden in a pillow.

At first he thought she might have fallen asleep, then he heard her sniffle as she raised her hand to wipe her eyes. Good Lord, he thought with the sense of helplessness a man feels when confronted with tears. She was crying.

Sitting down by her hip, he lifted her onto his lap. "Go ahead and cry, green eyes. I don't know anyone who has a better right."

"I'm not crying." Her voice was muffled against his chest.

His hand smoothed over her back, soothing yet arousing for both of them. "There must be a leak in the roof then, because my shirt seems to be wet."

She raised her head enough to look at his shirt. The light blue fabric was completely dry. Her head jerked up. "Your shirt isn't wet," she said, glaring at him.

"And you aren't crying any more," he said with satisfaction.

Before the sparks of her temper could flare into full flame, he lowered his head and kissed her in the way he'd wanted to since he had first seen her.

Passion overwhelmed her anger when he parted her lips. He had only to touch her and she came alive in a way she'd never thought possible. Strong hands flowed over her in a wave of heat, making her blood sing. Her breath dragged in her chest as he deepened the intimate caress of her mouth.

His touch became hard and urgent. He threaded his fingers through her soft hair to hold her as he rained kisses across her face. "Meredith," he breathed. "If I don't stop now, I won't be able to in a few minutes." He slid one arm down her side, his hand slipping under her denim skirt to find the bare skin underneath.

"Make that a few seconds," he growled.

Against her hip, she could feel how the kiss had affected him, and the knowledge that she could arouse him filled her with a primitive pleasure. Placing her hands on his chest, she raised her head, aware of his accelerated heartbeat beneath her palm.

"I can't tell you to stop," she whispered. "I know I should but I can't."

He closed his eyes. Need was clawing through him, deep and painful. "One of us is going to have to," he said, looking at her again. "I've just made several phone calls that are going to be bringing some people up here in a few minutes. As much as I would like to tell them all to go to hell, it's a little late now."

She started to squirm off his lap, but his arm tightened across her thighs. "Stay. We have a couple of minutes yet."

"If you're expecting people here, I should get out of your way. I can go to my room while you take care of business. Did you arrange for a room for me?"

"Yes."

There was a sharp tap at the door. "Tell me where it is and I'll leave."

Paul gently set her aside and stood up. Bringing her crutches over to her, he gestured toward a hallway off the living room. "It's the first door on the left."

"I'm not going to sleep with you," she said, wondering if he would believe her after the way she'd responded to his kiss. But reality had returned with the knock on the door. Paul had told her he wasn't interested in anything serious, and she didn't sleep with men casually.

"Then it's the second door on the left," he said.

Before she could tell him she didn't want to stay in his apartment at all, he had opened the door. First came a waiter pushing a cart laden with food. Paul pointed toward the dining room, and the waiter transferred the covered dishes from the cart onto the table.

While Paul was occupied with the waiter, Meredith tugged her skirt down and tucked the hem of her shirt back in. She attempted to tidy her hair by running her fingers through it, but there was nothing she could do about the turmoil inside her. Outwardly, no one would be aware of the aching emptiness that needed to be filled. At least, she hoped her emotions weren't as exposed as she felt. She schooled her features, but wasn't certain she could disguise the expression in her eyes.

A minute later there was another light knock on the door, and Paul let in a man who wore a utility belt and carried a telephone. After Paul instructed him where to put in the new phone, the installer set to work.

As the waiter left, Tulip entered, carrying a large wicker basket. The petite woman brought the basket over to Meredith. "I added a few items the hotel didn't furnish. After you look through everything, let me know what else you need."

Meredith glanced into the basket and saw an assortment of toiletries—soap, shampoo, toothpaste, toothbrush, moisturizing lotion.

Tulip sat down on the couch and opened a small notebook. "What kind of dog food does Ivan eat? What is his normal schedule? Are there any quirks or habits he has I should know about?"

Feeling dazed, Meredith answered Tulip's questions and watched her jot everything down in the notebook.

In the meantime, Paul was talking to two men who had arrived shortly after Tulip. He escorted them to the couch and introduced them to Meredith.

The tall, rangy man dressed in a brown leather vest worn open over a plaid shirt and jeans, was Michael Tray, Paul's friend who was a detective with the police department. The short man with him who sat down heavily in one of the chairs was Joe Falano, also a detective. His gray suit was rumpled, his tie slightly askew. His face had a weary hound-dog expression, and his sharp, intelligent eyes were in marked contrast to the rest of him.

Sitting down beside her, Paul informed the two detectives of the taped message from Meredith's sister and their visit to the club in Springfield. He didn't mention the money Laura had stolen. He just said they had reason to believe Meredith's sister was with Nichols, based on the facts that they had been dating before the theft and both disappeared at the same time.

Detective Tray pointed out there was no proof Laura was with Dan Nichols or an accomplice in the theft. She could have reasons of her own for making herself scarce for a few days. Perhaps she had had a quarrel with Nichols and needed time to lick her wounds. They needed something more to go on than a phone call from one sister to another.

Meredith waited for Paul to tell the detectives Laura had taken her money, but he didn't say a thing. So she did. She wanted her sister found before she got in any deeper than she already was.

"I don't think my sister knew about Nichols taking the money," she said, "but I do believe she's with him. It would be just the type of thing Laura would think was exciting, to run away with a man for the thrill of doing something different. She would even think it was romantic for a man to want to take her away from it all."

"What makes you think she wouldn't know about the theft?" Detective Faleno asked.

"My sister took some money out of my bank account before she left. If she had known Nichols had plenty of money, she wouldn't have felt it necessary to take mine."

"Do you have a picture of your sister?" Detective Tray asked. "It would help if we knew what she looked like."

"There are several photos of her in my apartment."

Before one of the detectives could ask her to get them, Paul explained about the smoke damage to her apartment. "A cleaning crew will be going there tomorrow morning. I'll have one of my staff locate the pictures and deliver them to you."

His hand moved to her thigh, effectively silencing any objections she might make. She could make all the protests she wanted later when they were alone.

The detectives seemed to be satisfied, and after a few more minutes of discussion they left.

"It takes a little getting used to, doesn't it?" Tulip said to Meredith as Paul walked the two men to the door.

"What does?"

Tulip smiled broadly. "You'll have to find out for yourself," she said cryptically, then added, "It might help if you remember the meaning of the word *rogue*. It fits. He's an animal with a savage nature that lives apart from the herd. If you expect him to act like other men with polite manners and romantic gestures, you're going to be disappointed."

Meredith's gaze went to the tall man opening the door for the detectives. "I'm not disappointed," she said quietly.

Approval and acceptance were in Tulip's eyes as she patted Meredith's hand. "Good. You'll do fine." Suddenly serious, Tulip offered another word of advice. "Loyalty means a great deal to Rogue. If he puts trust in someone, he expects to have it returned. He can be your best friend or your worst enemy, as Nichols will find out once Rogue catches up with him. He doesn't mind a good fight, but he always expects to win."

With that pronouncement completed, Tulip snapped her notebook shut. "Give me a call if you need anything." She rattled off her extension number as she stood up. "Don't worry about your dog, Meredith. I'll take very good care of him."

Meredith slumped back on the couch as Tulip swept out. For someone who had graduated at the top of her class, she was having a difficult time assimilating everything that had happened to her in the last couple of days. Somehow, she had lost control of her life, and she wasn't sure how to go about getting it back. Or even if she wanted to get it back.

The man who'd installed the phone reentered the living room. If he thought it was strange that Mr. Rouchett wanted a phone installed in a room where there was already a phone, he didn't make any comment. Paul let him out, then leaned back against the closed door, gazing at Meredith. A lot had been accomplished in a short while, but there was still more to be done. Like convincing Meredith to go along with his plans.

He fought the urge to smile, knowing she wouldn't appreciate his amusement. "Do you want to go to the table to eat, or would you like me to bring you a plate?"

She pressed her hand over her heart. "What?" she said in exaggerated surprise. "You're giving me a choice? Let me mark this down. The *Guinness Book of World Records* might be interested."

Crossing the room, he sat on the edge of the chair nearest to her and rested his forearms on his thighs. "There was a lot to get done in a brief period of time, Meredith. I have the staff and the connections to get them accomplished as soon as possible. You have enough to adjust to without needing the added burden of making decisions right now."

"Those decisions have to do with me, Paul. It's my apartment that is filled with smoke. It should be up to me to clean it and to find a place to stay in the meantime. You've got people going in to clean and to get the picture of my sister, and have provided me a place to stay."

"Since you're already mad, I might as well tell you what else I've done."

Crossing her arms over her chest, she stared at him and waited.

He sat back in the chair, stretching his legs out in front of him. "I had another phone installed which will have your number. Your answering machine will be hooked up to it in case your sister calls and we aren't here."

She was more angry with herself than with him because she hadn't thought of it first. "What else?" she asked, resigned.

Studying her closely to try to gauge the extent of her anger, he wondered if he was about to add fuel to the fire. "Tulip is going to be bringing you something to wear tonight. I thought we would have dinner at the club."

Remembering another man who had continually told her she wasn't dressed properly, she asked, "Why? Will you be ashamed of me if I'm not wearing what you've provided?"

"Don't be an idiot. You can wear a damn burlap bag for all I care and you would still be the most beautiful woman there. I thought you would be more comfortable knowing you were dressed appropriately."

She couldn't be offended even if she wanted to be. He had considered her feelings, not his. "Dammit. I wanted to stay angry with you. Instead, I find myself feeling I should be thanking you."

Again repressing a smile, he stood up and handed her the crutches. "You'll feel more yourself after you have something to eat. I don't know anyone who can argue very well on an empty stomach."

Meredith laughed. She couldn't help it. He was impossible, arrogant, and pushy. And she was very much afraid she was falling in love with him.

Six

There were other surprises in store for Meredith before the day was over.

They had just finished their snack when Tulip arrived with a large box. Luckily, Meredith was through eating because Tulip insisted she look at the dress she had bought for her.

Paul pushed back his chair and brought her crutches to her. "You might as well go along with her. It's easier and a lot quieter."

Tulip had gone ahead, and instead of taking the box into the guest room, she had laid it on Paul's bed. Meredith had been about to walk past his room when Tulip called her back. It unsettled her that Tulip naturally assumed she would be staying in the Rogue's bedroom. Maybe the swinging door should have been installed for his bedroom instead of the kitchen, she thought irritably. And she wasn't sure which bothered her more: Paul having a series of women or her not being sophisticated enough not to mind.

As she slowly made her way into Paul's bedroom, the crutches sank into plush gray carpet. Dark furniture hugged the off-white walls in a room larger than half of her apartment. A series of louvered doors ran along one wall, indicating a sizable closet. The room was neat and orderly except for a pair of cuff links on the long mahogany dresser. She couldn't help noticing there were no photos of family or friends.

One painting decorated the room. It was on the wall opposite the bed. She would have liked to be able to look at it more closely, but the rustle of tissue paper brought her attention back to Tulip.

Her mouth dropped open when she saw the dress Tulip lifted out of the box and held up. Considering Tulip's personal taste, Meredith had expected a rather conservative dress. That was not the word to describe the short strapless dress with rows of ruffles running from low on the hips to the above-the-knee hemline.

"Good Lord, Tulip," she said with chagrin. "I can't wear that."

"Of course you can. You aren't very big on top, but you have enough to keep the dress up."

Meredith choked back a laugh. "That's not exactly what I meant. I'm a nurse, not a showgirl, and in that dress I would definitely show more than I would be comfortable showing. Besides, with this cast on my leg, I'm going to look a little silly in that dress."

Tulip waved a hand dimissively. "When you show up in this dress, no one will notice your cast."

"It's what they will notice that bothers me."

Smiling, Tulip handed her the dress and patted her arm. "Don't you worry. Rogue will make sure no one bothers you." She giggled as she walked toward the door. "Except himself, of course."

"Wait. How much do I owe you for the dress?"

Tulip paused in the doorway and shook her head. "Not a penny. I charged it to Rogue. There are a few other little incidentals in the box I thought you might need. If you want anything else, just let me know."

Meredith could hear Tulip still chuckling as she walked down the hall. She didn't see what was so funny about the situation. She also didn't like thinking about the other women Tulip had provided clothing for in the past. From Tulip's casual attitude, Meredith got the impression buying other women's clothing was a normal part of her duties. She hadn't even asked Meredith's size. Examining the label, Meredith wasn't surprised the size was correct.

Leaning on her crutches, she held the dress up in front of her. What there was of it.

"Have you changed your mind?"

Her head jerked up. Paul was leaning against the frame of the door, his arms crossed. "About what?" she asked.

"This is my room, not the guest room."

"Tulip automatically assumed I would be staying with you. She brought the dress in here."

He pushed away from the door and crossed the room, stopping in front of her. "So *you* automatically assumed I entertain women in my bedroom on a regular basis."

Was that disappointment she heard in his voice, she wondered. His masculine scent drifted around her, captivating her. She tightened her grip on the dress, holding it against herself as if it were a shield.

His gaze lowered to the dress. "If that fits, I'm a dead man," he drawled.

"It's my size. Either Tulip is experienced in buying clothes for your . . . ah, guests or she has an exceptional eye for women's sizes."

Paul studied her expression. It was probably too much to hope she might be jealous. "She's never bought clothes for any women at my request, except for you." He tucked his finger under her chin and lifted her face so she had to look at him. "Would you like to know why?"

"It's none of my business."

A corner of his mouth curved upward. "Yes, it is." He stroked the backs of his fingers along the strong line of her jaw. "My reputation is based on an image, Meredith. I'm not the womanizer people like to think I am. They don't expect a man named Rogue to prefer a good book, soft music, and painting."

"You've been married twice, Paul. That isn't exactly being a monk."

He'd known the subject would come up eventually. He took the dress from her and tossed it onto the end of the bed. Then he urged her to sit on the bed beside him, dropping her crutches on the floor.

"My first marriage was when I was eighteen and my hormones were stronger than my good sense. It lasted three years. She got fed up with me working days and taking art courses at night. Any free time I had was spent in front of an easel, which she also resented. When she left, she took everything I had. At the time it wasn't much, but it took me a long time to work myself back to where I could continue my education."

He had taken possession of her hand, bringing it over to rest on his thigh. Threading his fingers through hers, he continued. "I packed away my paints and changed my major to business management. Shortly after I got my degree, I started a consulting business. I was determined never to be broke again. A year later I met a woman who was as ambitious as I. That time I approached marriage as though it were a business partnership. None of that romantic stuff for me. It was a practical relationship based more on financial statements than declarations of love. We bought a house in Chevy Chase because I thought it was a good investment, not because I wanted a place to raise a family." His mouth twisted ruefully. "Which was a good thing, because Janice wasn't interested in anything but making money. She worked for a pharmaceutical firm and her job required her to travel a great deal. Some of the work I did took me out of town on occasion. Days, even a week would go by without our seeing each other."

He was silent for a few minutes, seemingly lost in his thoughts as he stared down at their clasped hands.

"What happened?" she asked softly.

He raised his gaze to meet hers, finding gentle compassion in her eyes. "I ended up in the hospital with an ulcer. I was told I would be in serious trouble if I kept up the pace I had been maintaining. When I got out of the hospital, I made an appointment with Janice at her office and told her I wanted a divorce. At first she tried to talk me out if it, saying divorce would hurt her image with the company. When I told her I had sold my business and was going to concentrate on painting, she phoned her lawyer while I was still there."

Meredith glanced at the painting across the room. The man who had painted it had found peace with himself and his art. But at a price.

"How did you wind up owning a nightclub?"

His smile held a trace of self-mockery. "Starving in a garret isn't all it's cracked up to be. My ulcer kicked in again because I wasn't eating properly, and I knew I had to find a way to make a reasonable living and still be able to paint. The woman who owned the loft I had leased came by one day and asked if I would be interested in managing a nightclub she owned. I ended up buying it when Tulip decided to retire from the realty business."

"Tulip owned The Rogue's Den?"

He laughed softly. "Among other things. Her husband had left her with all his assets but no children. The nightclub was called The Dew Drop Inn and hadn't been managed very well. I redecorated it and booked some musicians. Tulip helped hire the staff in the beginning and ended up working full-time when she discovered retirement wasn't all it was cracked up to be."

Meredith had seen the affection in his eyes and heard it in his voice every time he mentioned Tulip. For a man who said he didn't want a family, he had one whether he realized it or not. She also understood why he was so adamant about finding Nichols. His ex-wives had taken everything he had worked for in the past. Nichols had stolen more than money from Paul. He had taken Paul's trust and ground it into the dirt.

Her gaze returned to the painting. "Where is your studio?"

"I still have the loft where I used to live." He lifted his hand and brushed a lock of her hair away from her cheek. "I usually don't do portraits, but I think I would like to paint you in that dress."

Humor flickered in her eyes. "You would have to use a lot of flesh tones. Tulip assures me that even though I'm not very big on top, I have enough to keep the dress up. I'm not as confident as she is."

His gaze lowered, and her breasts ached strangely, as though his hands were caressing her and not just his eyes. Heat seared through her as he ran his hand from her throat down to the swelling mound of her breast. Lifting his other hand, he caressed both breasts, molding them as though he were a sculptor rather than a painter.

He looked at her, the intensity of his dark gaze slamming into her. "You're perfect."

Desire tugged at her as his thumb stroked the hard tip of her breast. His name came out as though dragged from her, the sound one of growing hunger. It didn't matter who moved first to close the distance between them. The only important thing was desperate need to taste the ecstasy they found in each other.

He pressed her to the mattress, and she reveled in the glorious weight of his body partially covering hers. The dress fell off the end of the bed onto the floor, but neither noticed or cared.

She arched her spine and writhed as white-hot desire burst into flame. His hands and mouth fanned the fire inside her until she felt she would be burned up in the heat of passion.

He had trusted her with the story of his past. Now she trusted him with the intimacy of her naked skin as he swept her shirt away. Her teeth dug into her bottom lip to keep the delicious feeling from becoming a moan of pleasure as his tongue brushed across her breast.

"Don't," he groaned when he saw her white teeth embedded in her lip. "I can't stand it when you do that."

Opening her eyes, she saw his were blazing as he stared at her mouth. She released her lip as her hands slid around his back, bringing him down to her. She needed his solid strength against her aching breasts. Her fingers tugged his shirt free from his slacks, fighting to find the bare skin beneath it.

His weight was removed from her briefly as he tore his shirt open. When his heated flesh came in contact with her sensitive breasts, she was about to bite her lip again, but he prevented her by taking her mouth with his.

The combination of male hunger and tenderness clouded her mind with a passionate urgency to get closer, so close she wouldn't know where she stopped and he began.

His hand slipped between their bodies, pulling her skirt up so he could stroke her thigh. Her legs shifted, parted, and she arched suddenly in response to the intimate caress of his fingers. She felt as though she were going to explode, then was afraid she wouldn't.

Unaware she had bitten her lip again, she was startled when he murmured, "Don't hold back. Let me hear how you feel."

The last barriers of their clothing were swiftly stripped away. Flesh heated flesh. An aching sigh escaped Meredith as his hands flowed over her and his mouth followed. Desire quickened when Paul parted her legs and lowered his body to seek her warmth.

Urgent claws of a sensual trap gripped them and held on as they moved together, lost to everything around them. A spiraling tension tightened unbearably as they sought release, falling into the abyss of stunning pleasure when the trap opened and they fell through.

Locked together, they rode out the aftershocks. It was a long time before their breathing slowed and their heartbeats steadied.

Surprised he could move, Paul raised his head to look down at her. Her long lashes raised slowly to reveal her dazed eyes.

"Tell me what you're feeling," he said softly.

"Astonished."

Not because of her response, but because of the reason she had given herself over to the passion he created within her. She hadn't known she could be so totally immersed in someone else. But then, she had never been in love before. And that was what this had to be. No other word could describe her feeling except love. It might not make sense or be smart, but she couldn't deny it.

His eyes were dark with emotion. "I wanted this since I first heard your voice on the phone."

When she moved restlessly as though denying his words, she felt him harden inside her. She breathed his name. "Paul, I don't . . ."

"I have to have you again," he murmured, against her mouth, "to make sure you're real and not just a fantasy."

The incredible sequence began again, this time with less urgency but with an intensity as deep as darkness.

Exhausted, they fell asleep in each other's arms. The world would have to go on without them for a while.

Paul woke first. Easing his arm from under her, he raised up on one elbow, and looked down at her. He would like to paint her like this, he thought. He had never wanted to do a portrait before, preferring nature to people, but he found his fingers itching to hold a brush to convey her beauty and grace to canvas.

Her hair was mussed, the curls tangled around her face in glorious disarray. Her lips were still slightly swollen from his kisses, her skin porcelain-smooth and tinted with a healthy glow. The spread he had pulled around them before falling asleep left her shoulders bare and had slipped down to expose one breast.

His body tightened with the urge to taste her, to touch her, to take her again.

Leaving her required every ounce of his control, but he knew it was what he had to do. He didn't know what her reaction was going to be when she woke up. Making love to her again was only going to make it more difficult to leave her, if that was what she decided she wanted.

Not that he would be able to let her go, he realized. He needed her in a basic, elemental way he couldn't understand but could recognize. He would be able to give her some time to get used to their new relationship, but not much.

He slid out of bed and bent down for his clothes, gathering hers at the same time. Near his crumpled shirt was the dress Tulip had bought. He picked it up and arranged it over the back of a chair where Meredith would see it when she awoke. The dress box was also on the floor, and he noticed it wasn't empty. Tulip had thoughtfully provided shoes and hose as well. He laid them on the chair.

On his way around the bed, he stopped and allowed himself one more glimpse of her. She was where she should be—in his bed. She might say she didn't want to become involved with him, but it was too late. Her sensual response to him had been complete, with nothing held back. She might say she didn't want him, but she would be lying.

Maybe it was the sound of a door closing or the strangeness of her surroundings that woke Meredith. Opening her eyes, she glanced around the room, realizing immediately where she was. Her body ached a little when she stretched, reminding her of how she had ended up in Paul's bed.

Even before she turned her head on the pillow, she knew she was alone.

She told herself she should be feeling relief instead of regret that Paul had left the bed. She wasn't sure what her reaction would be when she faced him again, and she was eager to know what his would be.

If he was casual about taking her to his bed, she would want to die.

Tossing back the spread, she rolled over to look down at the floor. By some miracle, her crutches were right beside her. It would have been embarrassing if she had been stranded on his bed or been caught crawling across the floor. Especially since she didn't have a stitch on.

As she sat up, she saw the dress draped over a chair across the room. Paul hadn't said what time they would be going to the club, but she needed all the confidence she could muster to face him again. The dress might just keep him off balance enough for her to find hers. If the darn thing didn't fall off her.

She smiled. Considering his reaction to her naked body earlier, that would definitely keep him off balance.

When Paul returned from the loft, he was going to take a shower, but his bathroom was occupied. He was startled to realize he liked his privacy being invaded, something he usually prized highly.

He liked the idea of Meredith rubbing the soap he used over her skin, using his towels to pat the drops of moisture off her breasts, her slender waist, and hips.

He groaned silently. Just thinking about her drove him crazy. The hardening of his body had him striding quickly to the shower in the guest room. First he was going to turn the cold water on full blast.

Fifteen minutes later he came out of the guest bathroom with a towel wrapped around his hips. His bedroom and bathroom were both empty when he entered. The bed had been made; the dress and the shoes were gone. One of his shirts was casually draped over the end of the bed, and he picked it up. Her scent rose to cloud his senses, making his fingers tighten on the shirt. He liked the thought of her wearing one of his shirts after she left his bed.

Dammit, he cursed under his breath. Where in hell was she?

His bare feet sank into the carpet as he strode through the living room, dining room, and finally the kitchen. Meredith wasn't anywhere.

He looked at his watch. It was almost seven. Fighting the panic welling up inside him, he grabbed the phone in the kitchen and punched out Tulip's extension. When she answered on the second ring, he asked, "Where is she?"

Tulip laughed. "Hello, Rogue. Correct me if I'm wrong, but I assume you mean Miss Claryon."

"You know damn well who I mean. Has she called you? Have you seen her?"

"Hold your horses. She came down to check on her dog. Then she wanted to know how Mr. Bowers was, so I had Baxter bring him down. They're in the club at your table. I just left them. That Jeremiah Bowers is a sweetie. As far as I know, she's still there."

"You left her there alone?"

"Oh, she's not alone," Tulip replied, vastly amused. "She has a lot of company."

His fingers tightened around the phone. "Tell me she's not wearing that dress."

"I thought you liked that dress."

"I do. I just don't want her wearing it in public if I'm not with her."

"I was counting on that."

Paul's mind was on Meredith and not on what Tulip way saying, so he missed the satisfaction in her voice. "You go stay with her until I get there."

"But—"

"Now, Tulip."

He heard her giggling before the line went dead. Slamming the phone down, he left the kitchen.

Meredith was laughing at something Tulip was saying when Paul walked up to the table. He could tell the moment she saw him. Her eyes changed, warmth replacing amusement.

The two men who had been hovering in the background melted away the moment Paul shifted his steely gaze in their direction. He looked down at the table and counted four full cocktail glasses in front of Meredith. He could only hope the waiters were giving the rest of the patrons the fantastic service they were giving her.

He couldn't blame the other men for ogling her. And it wasn't just the dress, although the display of her smooth bare flesh was definitely an attraction. He wanted to throw his tuxedo jacket around her shoulders so the other men wouldn't stare at her.

She was his. The sooner everyone realized that, the better it would be for all concerned.

Before he pulled out his chair, he took her hand and kissed her palm. He ignored Tulip's wide smile as he sat down next to Meredith. He couldn't ignore her conversation, however.

"Now you don't have to put a sign up or take out an ad in the newspaper," Tulip said lightly. "I think everyone got the message."

His smile held a trace of self-mockery. "It was either that or have Baxter wrap barbed wire around this table. Do you need some help with Meredith's dog, or can you get him home by yourself?"

"He's a pussycat. I won't have any trouble with him." Tulip leaned over and patted Meredith's arm. "That's my cue to leave. Remember what I said. It's good advice."

Meredith smiled. "I'll remember. I hope Ivan doesn't give you too much trouble, Tulip. I appreciate your taking care of him. I hope it won't be for long."

Pushing back her chair, Tulip glanced at Paul. "I'll keep him as long as it takes."

Meredith frowned as she watched Tulip leave the nightclub. Bringing her gaze back to Paul, she asked, "What does she mean? As long as what takes?"

"She's just rambling." He brought her hand to his mouth again. "What advice did she give you?"

His warm breath caressed her skin, sending a different kind of heat through her veins. "She was just rambling."

He smiled. She could give as good as she got. Suddenly serious, he said, "We should talk about this afternoon."

She nodded. Some questions had been answered

when he had kissed her hand, but there were more. "I'm paying for this dress."

If she had thrown one of the drinks in his face, he couldn't have been more surprised. "You don't have to pay for it. It was my idea."

Leaning forward, she covered their clasped hands with her free one. "I do have to pay for it. Otherwise, I would feel it was some sort of payment for going to bed with you."

His eyes darkened with some undefined emotion. "That isn't why I wanted you to have the dress, Meredith." His gaze lowered to the swell of her breasts above the strapless top. "If the dress bothers you so much, we can return to my room. I'd be more than happy to take it off you."

A faint flush tinted her cheeks as the molten heat of desire erupted again in her lower body. The blood in her veins seemed heavy and hot, and her breath caught in her throat at the look in his eyes.

"You are a rogue, Paul," she said softly, her gaze locking with his.

He shook his head. "I'm only a man, green eyes. One who wants you very badly."

A male voice intruded on their conversation. "Meredith?" When she looked up, the man added, "I thought it was you. How are you? I heard you had some sort of accident. Apparently it wasn't that serious."

"Hello, Eric," she said stiffly. It was an effort to appear polite.

Since she wasn't going to do the honors, he extended his right hand toward Paul. "I'm Eric Thomasville, aide to Senator Cameron."

Paul shook the other man's hand, giving only his name. He hid his amusement as Eric Thomasville examined him closely, taking in the tuxedo and his and Meredith's clasped hands resting on the table. Men like Eric Thomasville were common in the nation's capital. Tall with expertly styled dark hair and wearing an expensive but discreet suit, he exuded the clammy friendliness unique to the political arena.

And the guy seemed to know Meredith very well.

Since Paul hadn't volunteered the information about himself, Eric asked, "Are you a relative of Meredith's? I don't remember her mentioning your name."

"I'm not a relative."

The other man again glanced at Paul's tuxedo. "Do you work here?"

"Paul owns The Rogue's Den, Eric," Meredith said, knowing Eric would be suitably impressed. "I'm surprised to see you here. If I remember correctly, you once said Old Town was passé, or words to that effect."

Leaning forward, Eric spoke in a low voice as though confiding a great secret. "Valencia heard Senator Cameron's secretary rave about this club. Apparently, it's a favorite watering hole for some of the Secret Service and FBI boys."

Meredith flicked a glance at Paul, smiling faintly. "High praise, indeed. Say hello to Valencia for me."

Eric straightened and nodded. "If we hadn't already ordered, I would ask you to join us, but perhaps another time." Suddenly, he snapped his fingers as though something had just occurred to him. "By the way, I saw someone you know yesterday. Or was it the day before? No, it was yesterday. I had one of those days, you understand. Late for a luncheon, meetings piled on top of each other, you know how it is. When the congressman wants things done, he wants them done right now or sooner."

Meredith was only half listening to Eric's self-important litany. "Whom did you see?"

"It was at one of the marinas. I forget which one. We were on our way to have lunch with Valencia's father at the Yacht Club and somehow took a wrong turn somewhere. I stopped to ask directions from a couple who were unloading their car and discovered the woman was your sister Laura." He added with a ghost of a laugh, "She didn't seem especially pleased to see me. Was she off for an illicit weekend?"

Meredith had stiffened at her sister's name. Not wanting Eric to know how important his offhand remark was, she tried to keep her voice casual. "Why do you think Laura was going away?"

He shrugged. "She and the man she was with had enough supplies to last them several weeks. They were loading them onto a thirty-foot sailboat. I asked her if they were going to sail to the Bahamas, and she just laughed and said they weren't going quite that far. I didn't get a chance to ask her what their destination was, because her friend called to her from the boat to hurry her up."

Meredith and Paul exchanged looks. Before they could ask for more details, Eric reached into his inside coat pocket and withdrew a leather case. Taking out a white business card, he handed it to Paul. "Give me a call sometime. We'll have lunch. I must get back to Valencia. It's good seeing you again, Meredith."

As Eric sauntered off, Meredith watched Paul slowly tear the business card in half before dropping it into an ashtray.

Mischief danced in her eyes. "You don't want to have lunch with Eric?"

"Not in this lifetime. What kind of a name is Valencia? It sounds like a set of luggage."

"I believe that's her professional name." She chuckled when he raised a brow. "She's a fashion model. You might not approve of his choice in dinner companions, but if it weren't for Eric, we wouldn't know Laura and Nichols are floating around somewhere on a boat. I can't believe I forgot about the boat."

She leaned forward, laying her arms on the table. Paul discovered he was more interested in staring at the tempting rise of her breasts than in hearing about her sister and a sailboat. "Laura has always lived beyond her means," Meredith said. "When she lived at home, she was forever six months ahead on her allowance. She spends her salary the moment she gets it. One of her more elaborate purchases this year was investing in a boat along with two women she works with. Only one of them knows how to sail, but Laura liked the thought of owning a boat so she could wander around on deck in her bikini."

Paul lifted his hand to summon a waiter. "Now all we have to do is find one boat out of the thousands between here and the Bahamas."

"Eric said they weren't going that far. I can ask the other women who co-own the boat if they know where Laura might be going."

Considering that all he had thought about for the past week was finding Nichols, Paul was surprised he didn't feel like following up on this latest development right away. He gazed intently at her. "Thomasville seems to think he knows you well. Why is that?"

Meredith blinked. It wasn't the question she had expected him to ask. She was tempted to brush off Eric as easily as Eric had brushed off her pride, but Paul had been honest about his past. He deserved the same from her.

"I met Eric at a party Laura dragged me to one night about a year ago. It was at a lovely house in Georgetown. I still don't know how Laura managed to get us invited, but a lot of people there knew her. At first when Eric asked me out, I was flattered. We went to the finest places, usually in limousines, met important people, and dined on exotic foods. Rubbing elbows with senators and congressmen was pretty heady stuff for a farm girl from Nebraska."

The waiter came up to their table, and Paul murmured something to him. When they were alone again, he asked, "So when did you get tired of rubbing elbows with the elite?"

She laughed shortly. "When both my capacity for boredom and my bank account gave out. It's hard to maintain on a nurse's salary the kind of wardrobe that life-style requires. I also got tired of Eric telling me I was dressed incorrectly or I shouldn't laugh out loud in public."

"Did you sleep with him?"

Fury flashed in her eyes. "Don't let anything like good manners stand in your way, Mr. Rouchett. Be as blunt and outspoken as you like."

"I will. You didn't answer my question. Did you sleep with him?"

He was as relentless as a dentist's drill, she thought. "No," she said crossly. "I didn't sleep with him. It wasn't that type of relationship."

"Don't tell me you were just buddies, Meredith. Unless the man is a eunuch, and having met him,

I admit that could very well be a possibility, he would want to take you to bed."

She pulled her hand away and clenched it in her lap. Humiliation and hurt made her voice husky. "And you think he must have been successful because you were?"

"Don't be a fool. You know that's not what I think."

"I have been a fool, haven't I? I made it so easy for you, so therefore I must be easy."

Before he could respond, the waiter came back to the table holding a piece of paper, but Paul waved him away. Meredith took advantage of the interruption to push back her chair and reach for her crutches. She would have loved to storm out of the club on two solid feet, but she was going to have to settle for clopping out on crutches.

She heard him call her name, but she didn't stop. She had to get away from him. Earlier, she had wondered what he thought about her sharing his bed. Now she knew.

Seven

Meredith didn't realize Paul was behind her until she had stepped outside the club. When the cool night air hit her bare skin, she shivered. She hadn't the faintest idea where she was going, but she was going to have to make up her mind soon. She wasn't exactly dressed for an evening stroll, unless she planned on becoming a streetwalker.

Startled when a tuxedo jacket was draped over her shoulders, she jerked away from Paul's hands. "I don't want your coat. I don't want anything from you."

"Don't be stupid. It's cold out here."

"A minute ago I was an idiot. Now I'm stupid. I wish I could disagree with your gracious description of my mental faculties, but at the moment they couldn't be more accurate."

"Then stop acting like a fool and come back inside. We need to talk."

They were at the front entrance of the hotel when Meredith stopped walking and faced him. She shrugged her shoulders so that his coat fell to the ground. "I'm not going back to your apartment. I should never have gone there in the first place."

He picked up his coat and replaced it across her shoulders. "All right. We won't go to my apartment, but keep this on."

"I'm really tired of your telling me what to do."

"That's it," he muttered under his breath, coming to the end of his patience.

In one smooth motion he slid his arm under her knees and lifted her. The crutches clattered to the sidewalk, and he stepped over them. Over his shoulder, he yelled, "Ralph, take the crutches inside. She's not going to need them."

Whether the doorman did as he asked or not, Paul couldn't have cared less. He continued walking away from the hotel. Meredith struggled at first, but stopped when he ignored her.

On the other side of the hotel parking lot was a small warehouse. At the door Paul shifted her in his arms so he could have one hand free to work the electronic lock. There was a click, and he shoved the door open with his shoulder. Easing her through the doorway, he immediately headed for the stairs in front of them.

His footsteps sounded hollow on the wooden landing as he crossed to another door and again punched out a combination on another electronic lock.

After closing the door behind them, he flicked a switch with his elbow. Lights flooded a large, cavernous room. Meredith caught a glimpse of bare rafters high in the ceiling and thick support posts from floor to the roof. She was unable to see anything else until he lowered her onto a plump divan.

Holding on to his coat, she looked around. She was seated in a small area where there was the divan, a rocking chair, and a shelf unit holding a stereo, a small television, and books. All were arranged around a large faded Oriental rug spread out on the dusty wooden floor.

A short distance away she saw a large studio easel with a canvas on it covered by a cloth. Next to it were containers of paintbrushes, tubes of paint on a tray, and a palette lying on a square table. Unframed paintings were stacked facing the wall.

Now she knew where she was. This was Paul's studio.

Her anger had evaporated. Weariness laid over her like a thick wool blanket, smothering her. "Why did you bring me here, Paul?"

He yanked off his tie and unfastened the two top buttons of his dress shirt as though it were strangling him. "You didn't want to go back to my apartment. We can't very well go to yours. We could have driven around for the rest of the night, but I feel I might want my hands free to strangle you."

"Why?" she asked, her eyes widening in surprise. "Just because I finally came to my senses?"

He sat down in the wooden rocker, stretching his long legs out in front of him. He looked as exhausted as she felt. "Is that what you call it? I'd call it losing your mind."

She flopped back on the divan. "You might be right," she said with a sigh. "I certainly haven't shown a great deal of intelligence the last couple of days."

His gaze rested on the soft rise of her breasts, visible through the gap of his coat. With a great deal of control he dragged his mind back to their argument, even though he ached to tear the dress off her and feel her satiny skin heat beneath his hands.

"Are you regretting making love with me?" he asked.

"No," she said quietly. "I don't."

Rarely nervous, he didn't recognize how tense he was until he heard her answer. "Are you upset because we haven't known each other very long before we made love?"

She shook her head.

Exasperation tightened his jaw. He had eliminated some possible causes for her anger. There was one left. "I don't think you've slept around, Meredith. That isn't what I meant when I asked you about Thomasville. I asked because I couldn't stand the thought of your being with any other man. I've never been jealous before. You'll have to excuse me if I don't handle it very well."

Bewildered, she stared at him. "You were jealous?"

"I don't know what else to call it. It's the only reason I can think of for wanting to throw him out of the club just because he knew you."

"Paul," she said hesitantly, wondering how to make him clarify his feelings for her. She decided to repeat the rules they had made earlier about their relationship to see if he still felt that way. "You said you didn't want to get involved. Jealousy doesn't sound like part of an uninvolved relationship."

He came over to the divan and knelt in front of her, covering her hands with his. "I don't know what this is, Meredith. What I do know is that I want to find out."

She shook her head as though denying what he

was saying. "Everything is happening too quickly, Paul. What about your search for Nichols?"

"I'll find him."

"Then there's my apartment."

"It'll be cleaned."

"I have a broken ankle."

"It will heal."

She frowned at him. "You have an answer for everything, don't you?"

As he stood up, he tugged at her hands, bringing her to stand in front of him. "Not all of them. That's what I've been trying to tell you. I don't know why I want you so badly, why I find it impossible not to touch you."

She slowly closed her eyes as his lips brushed over the sensitive skin under her ear, then grazed across her flesh to the rise of her breasts. Even as she protested, her body yielded to the demands of his.

"Paul, this doesn't accomplish anything."

He gazed down at her. "Open your eyes. Look at me, Meredith."

Almost reluctantly, she raised her lashes and faced him.

"Tell me you don't want this, and I'll stop. It will be one of the hardest things I've ever had to do in my life, but I'll stop. All you have to do is say you don't want my hands on you, that you don't want me stroking your body inside and out."

Her resistance ebbed away at the tide of emotion his words created deep inside her. He was making love to her with his voice. Then his hands moved to the zipper of her dress, and she was lost.

• • •

An hour later Meredith was sitting on the divan wearing Paul's dress shirt. He had unearthed a pair of jeans and a denim shirt, which he had left partially unbuttoned. He had also found some food in a small refrigerator. Along with salami and cheese, he brought out a bottle of wine, pouring the golden liquid into two jelly glasses with cartoon figures on the sides.

Sitting with her good leg under her and her casted foot resting across his thighs, she lifted her glass to make a toast. "Here's to Fred and Wilma Flintstone. They always have a happy ending."

Paul started to draw on her cast with a black felt-tip pen. "I'm more into happy beginnings with the occasional bouts of contentment in between episodes of problems followed by peace and a happy ending."

"Which category do I fall into?" she asked quietly.

He stopped drawing and looked up at her. The collar of his shirt was turned up around her delicate throat. Her hair was mussed from his fingers running through it when they had made love. There was a soft glow in the depths of her eyes, and he liked to think he had put it there.

He smiled. "We've already had the happy beginning, and we'll work out the problems. Who knows, we might even have a happy ending."

Meredith wondered what his version of a happy ending was. She could have asked, but she really didn't want to know. Not then. Not when she was still wrapped in the warmth of his lovemaking. She didn't want to know when their relationship was going to end. When it did, it certainly wouldn't be a happy ending for her.

He put the cap back on the pen and patted her

cast. "There. It won't be hung in the Louvre, but it will serve the purpose."

She sat forward so she could see the cast. He had drawn a caricature of his face, complete with a black eye patch over one eye and a bandanna around his head. It was the logo of the club.

It was also a statement of possession.

"Very nice," she murmured. She was tempted to tell him that she was going to have the cast cut off soon, and she would no longer be wearing his trademark.

"Have you always wanted to be an artist, Paul?"

His eyes registered his surprise at the change of subject, then he shrugged. "I don't know the exact moment I realized painting was a necessity and not just a hobby. For as long as I can remember, I would draw on whatever I could find; grocery sacks, the backs of envelopes, even in the frost that formed on the window in my bedroom. When I was older and could make money mowing lawns, I would buy pads of typing paper. It wasn't until I took an art class in high school that I learned the right kind of paper and pencils to buy."

"Did your parents think it was a waste of money to buy you what you needed?"

His finger traced the lines he had drawn on her cast. "My father was an alcoholic. His paycheck went for booze."

That explained why he didn't drink hard liquor, she thought. "And your mother?" she asked quietly.

"My father said she died when I was three."

"Where's your father now?"

"He died when I was fifteen, which meant I had to work after school to support myself."

"You've been on your own since you were fifteen?" she exclaimed in shock.

"More or less." He smiled faintly when he caught her expression. "It's not really all that terrible, green eyes. I was on my own even when my father was alive."

She wrapped her arms across her middle, suddenly cold at the thought of how alone he had been for so long. "I had the opposite childhood. It seemed I was always with my parents. Their farm is a long way from any neighbors, and my father is very shy, so we didn't socialize much on the rare occasions we all went into town. We were always together, except when Laura and I went to school. It was as if we lived in tandem, working together, eating together."

"How did they feel about you and Laura moving so far away?"

Shadows of sadness darkened her eyes. "My mother understood. My father didn't. I think she would have liked to have gotten away, too, if she could. She writes to us, but my father won't have anything to do with either of us."

He grasped her hand. "Good Lord. Did he expect you and your sister to stay on the farm forever?"

"Yes. That's exactly what he expected."

Paul stared at her for a long moment, understanding now her thorny independence. She would depend only on herself rather than run the risk of someone else deciding how she should live. He silently promised her he wouldn't do that. He only wanted to make her life easier.

"Move over," he ordered gently, shifting her cast off his lap.

"Why?"

"Because tomorrow is going to be a very busy day, and we both could use some sleep."

She grunted as he tugged her down until she was lying on the couch. "Here?"

"I have a perfectly good bed in my apartment, but you don't want to go back there. This is better than the floor." Stretching out next to her, he found himself perilously near the edge. "Not much better than the floor but softer."

She rolled onto her side to give him more room. "Okay," she said agreeably.

Chuckling, he slid his arm under her, lifting her until she was lying on top of him. "Just like that? No argument?"

Resting her arms on his chest, she smiled. "Do you want one?"

"No." His hands slid under the hem of the shirt to find her bare bottom. "There are a lot of things I want to do with you. Arguing isn't one of them."

The magic she found with him began to weave its spell once more. "I thought you were tired."

"I never said I was tired. Just that we should get some sleep because we're going to be busy tomorrow."

"You're doing it again."

He ground her hips into his aroused lower body. "I know," he said softly.

It wasn't easy to think clearly when he was touching her like that. "I meant you make plans for me but you don't tell me what they are. I have a college degree, am a registered nurse, and can balance my checkbook down to the last penny. I can keep a secret and I don't gossip. I have been known to make decisions for myself, and except for the last few days have managed to take care of myself without any help."

She was trying hard to tell him something, he realized, but he was losing interest in conversation. His need for her eclipsed everything else, even his search for Nichols, something he thought could never happen.

His fingers stroked and clutched. "I don't remember asking for references."

"I don't remember you ever giving me choices either. You've just sort of taken over. Maybe I won't like the plans you've made for tomorrow."

He smiled as her hips undulated provocatively under the pressure of his hands. She was undeniably the most sensual woman he had ever known. And she didn't even realize it. That was part of the attraction.

He didn't want to talk any longer. "I'm not going to tell you what I've planned for tomorrow in case you don't like it. I don't feel like having a debate with you when all I can think about is making love with you."

Her hands swept across his chest, teasing and tantalizing. She brushed his lips with her tongue. "We'll argue in the morning."

They made an odd spectacle when they entered the hotel the next morning. Wearing his jeans and denim shirt, Paul didn't look as odd as Meredith. The tail of his dress shirt flapped against the ruffles of her dress as he carried her through the lobby toward the elevator. It was extremely difficult to appear to have any sort of dignity.

This time Meredith didn't complain about going to his apartment. In fact, she could hardly wait to get there and away from all the curious stares and giggles. Especially the giggles.

Once inside his apartment, he set her down in a chair. "Does Ralph the doorman still have my crutches?"

"I'll call down and have them sent up."

She frowned. "I don't care if every stitch of clothing I own stinks like an overcooked turkey. I need some clothes. I can't wear this all day."

Paul began to unbutton his shirt. "Call Tulip. She'll pick up whatever you need at the dress shop up the street. Just tell her what you want. I'm going to take a shower."

Meredith had never been particularly vain about her appearance, as her sister was. Since she usually spent most of her days in a white uniform, her taste in clothing ran to casual comfort over current styles when she wasn't at the hospital.

Still, she wasn't wild about looking ridiculous either.

So what else was she going to do? she asked herself, looking down at her strapless dress and his dress shirt. It wasn't that she had a lot of options. Unless she wanted to go around looking like the leftovers from a party, she was going to have to ask Tulip to shop for her again. This time, though, she was going to give specific instructions as to what to buy.

Several different styles of clothing ran through her mind. All she had to do was describe what she wanted, giving color, size, and design. No problem.

"She really doesn't like me, Paul," Meredith said, moaning. "I've never done anything to offend her that I know of, but I'm sure she doesn't like me."

Paul walked around her, keeping a straight face

with great effort while he carefully examined her outfit. "You look very . . . nice."

She scowled. "That's almost as good as saying I look interesting." She plucked at the oversize sweater. "This isn't quite what I had in mind when I asked Tulip to buy me a conservative white sweater and a black skirt."

Stopping in front of her, he lifted the neckline of the sweater back onto her shoulder. It fell down again, exposing her shoulder. "It's white and it's a sweater."

"It's also three sizes too big."

His gaze lowered to her skirt. "The skirt is black."

"Paul, it's made out of leather and it's indecently short."

He couldn't help it. She was so indignant and so darned cute when she was mad. Laughing, he reached out and pulled her into his arms.

She snuggled against his chest. "I'm afraid to look at the other things she's bought." Raising her head, she said, "But I'm going to pay you back for all you've spent on them."

"I'll send you a bill," he said lightly.

Great, she thought, smiling weakly. She could add it to all the others in her kitchen drawer. "So now that I'm fashionably attired, I'm ready to go to North Carolina."

"Are you sure that's where your sister has gone?"

"That's what one of the co-owners of the boat said. Laura called her a couple of days ago asking if Cindy's parents were at their cottage in Nags Head. When Cindy said it was vacant, Laura asked if she could use it for a week or so. She picked up the key and the directions two days ago. Now, I know I'm not Dick Tracy, but it seems to me it's obvious that they're heading for Nags Head."

"I would think it would be easier to drive down rather than sail, but Nichols might think the police would have his license plate number, and you said your sister's car isn't working."

She grinned at him. "We turned out to be pretty good detectives after all, didn't we? We have the address from Cindy, so all we have to do is go to Nags Head and seize our two thieves."

He kissed her nose. "While you were sloshing around in the shower with a trash bag wrapped around your leg, I called the airport. Unfortunately, there's a tropical storm warning for that area, so we can't fly down. We'll have to drive."

"Maybe Laura arranged for the boat and they went through the charade of loading it, but it's a trick to throw off anyone following them. They're actually going in the opposite direction."

"I don't think so. No offense, but your sister is not the stuff great crooks are made of. Unless I'm mistaken, Laura thinks he wanted the boat so they could take a romantic boat ride."

"You don't think she knows about Nichols stealing your money?"

He shook his head. "If she did, she would have no reason to clean out your bank account."

It was what she had told the detectives. Now she knew Paul agreed with her. It would be just like Laura to take her money to buy new clothes so she could impress a man. One thing that had bothered her was that Laura wasn't the type to get involved in anything illegal. She might be flighty and irresponsible about some things, but she wasn't dishonest. Taking her sister's money wouldn't fit into the same category as an accountant stealing from his employer.

"There's so much to do," she said, "and you

want to go hurrying off to North Carolina on what could be a wild-goose chase. I need to supervise the cleaning of my apartment."

"No, you don't. I hired the best. They'll leave it immaculate."

Of course he hired the best, she thought. "I should see how Mr. Bowers is."

"He's fine, happily immersed in cleaning his trains."

"Ivan?"

"The report I got this morning from Tulip is he was happily chasing a ball in her backyard when she left." He slid his hand over her shoulder, enjoying the feel of her silky skin. "Anything else?"

Resigned, she gave in. "I guess that's all. Let's go to North Carolina."

After the long six-hour drive, they stopped at a restaurant on the outskirts of Nags Head for a late lunch. Paul made a few phone calls while they waited for their order. When he returned, he informed her he had managed to rent a small cottage several houses away from the one her sister was supposed to be in.

Leaning toward Meredith, he disregarded his sandwich. "The realtor said there have been several cancellations because of the predicted storm. She was more than happy to let us have the place for a few days."

She noted his thoughtful expression. "You don't appear very pleased about that."

"It's too easy. Dan Nichols is an intelligent man. He didn't just decide one day to pilfer funds from my business. A great deal of planning was behind every move he made over a long period of time. It doesn't make sense that he would leave such an obvious trail that we could follow. He's smarter than that."

"Not if he isn't aware we know Laura is with him," Meredith said casually, and bit into her pickle.

Paul stared at her. She had cut through all the confusion and come up with the answer. "You might be right." He threw money on the table and handed her the crutches. "Let's go find out."

While they had been in the restaurant, the weather had changed drastically. A gust of wind jerked the door out of Paul's hand as he held it open for Meredith. It slammed against the outside wall of the restaurant before he could stop it. It wasn't raining yet, but the dark clouds overhead looked ominous.

Even though it was only the middle of the afternoon, Paul had to turn on the headlights as they drove to the realtor's. While they were there, Paul asked the woman to phone the number he gave her and ask for Laura Claryon. He told the woman they wanted to surprise Meredith's sister, which was why they didn't make the call themselves. If the realtor thought the request was a peculiar one, she humored him and made the phone call. There was no answer.

As they drove to the cottage, the weather worsened. Tree limbs and traffic lights swung violently as the wind buffeted them, and once Paul had to swerve to miss a plastic trash can rolling across the road.

They drove by the place where Laura was supposed to be, but it was dark.

Meredith craned her neck to look at the house as they passed. "Maybe they changed their minds."

"Or they haven't gotten here yet. You said yourself Laura doesn't know how to sail. I don't know how experienced Nichols is. He wasn't one to talk much about himself. This weather can't be helping if they're out on the water."

"You don't think they could be in danger, do you?"

"If there's one thing Nichols prizes more than money, it's his skin. He would pull into port somewhere if the weather was going to threaten them. Or they could be here already and simply gone out shopping or sightseeing."

The realtor had called it a cottage, but they discovered it was a sprawling four-bedroom house complete with fireplaces in the living room and two of the bedrooms. Luckily, it hadn't been constructed on stilts as a lot of the houses in that area were, so Meredith didn't have to try to navigate stairs.

The view was magnificent, which made up for the lack of furnishings. Apparently, the owners had decided to leave only what was necessary, taking the frills like lamps, rugs, and light bulbs away. Meredith had to be careful with her crutches on the bare wood floors as she made her way to the large window.

It had started to rain, the water streaming down the glass, blurring their view of the ocean. There were windows only on the side facing the ocean, as though that was the only scene worth viewing. With the wind buffeting the house and only one lamp to illuminate the room, it was intimate and cozy. Meredith could almost believe they were the only people in the world.

Although furnishings were sparse, they were adequate. The one thing they hadn't thought about, though, was food.

Coming out of the kitchen, Paul walked over to

her. "I know you won't like this, but it will be easier if I go get us some food and you stay here."

She started to turn to protest, but one of the crutches slipped on the floor. He steadied her as she muttered a curse under her breath.

Paul couldn't blame her for not liking the situation. He wouldn't under the same circumstances. "If there wasn't a storm, we could take our time, Meredith. But the storm is getting worse, and you and your cast will be drenched the minute you get out the door. This way I can get what we need, and you'll be safe and dry here."

"I know," she said grumpily. "I just feel so useless, and it's not a feeling I like. I'm being more of a burden to you than helping in any way."

He bent down and kissed her lightly. "It won't be for much longer."

Meredith frowned, watching him as he turned up the collar of his jacket and left the cottage. He could have meant she wouldn't be wearing the cast much longer, wouldn't be having to chase down Nichols and Laura much longer . . .

Or they wouldn't be together much longer.

Eight

The storm had grown in its intensity, heightening Meredith's concern. She wasn't nervous about storms generally, but she was worried about Paul being out in the bad weather.

She also couldn't help wondering if her sister was safe. This was one situation Laura couldn't get out of by a simple apology or a pretty smile and a shrug.

When Paul finally returned to the cottage, he was soaked to the skin and carrying a bag of groceries in each arm. The sacks were more wet than dry, with some of the groceries poking out through the sodden brown paper.

It took him two more trips to the car to bring in the things he had bought. Meredith hobbled into the kitchen, which was divided from the living room by a large counter where he had placed the bags. She began taking the food out of the sacks while he brought in the suitcase they'd hastily packed before leaving Alexandria.

There seemed to be enough food for a small

army, which made Meredith wonder how long Paul thought they were going to have to stay in Nags Head.

As he joined her in the kitchen, the lights suddenly blinked, then went out completely. "Don't move, Meredith," he said quickly, afraid she would stumble in the dark. "Stay where you are until I find the candles I bought."

They searched through the sacks, feeling for the box of candles and matches. Meredith tried to guess what some of the items were she picked up, and her bizarre choices had Paul laughing.

As her fingers traveled over a plastic-wrapped package, she wondered if it was cheese or lunch meat. "It's going to be real interesting to see how we manage to cook some of this food with the electricity out."

Crisp paper rattled as Paul picked up a bag of potato chips. "The lights in the grocery store were flickering occasionally, so I threw in the candles and some junk food just in case we had to rough it."

Finally, when a flash of lightning briefly illuminated the room, she found a box containing six candles. "Now we need to find matches."

While sweeping his hand across the counter, Paul felt a familiar object. "Our generous landlord must have missed these when he stripped the place."

Meredith chuckled as she held out a candle for him to light. "He isn't a very trusting soul, is he? I noticed the lamp is bolted to the table."

"Some of the furniture is anchored to the floor too. Evidently, the owner has had some bad experiences with tourists." When the candle was lighted, he could see her face in the faint glow.

"I'm sorry about the accommodations, Meredith. It was the best I could do on such short notice."

She smiled. "It's fairly clean, definitely dry, and we have running water. What more could we want?"

"I could think of a number of things," he said dryly. "Like a comfortable bed and a hot meal. There aren't any sheets for the beds, and I'm not up to cooking over an open fire."

Holding out another candle, she teased, "You're getting soft, Rogue. This is better than camping out on the cold ground or sleeping in the car."

She could have added the most important part— they were together.

A few seconds later, three candles were illuminating the kitchen. Ten minutes after that, there was a flickering fire in the living room fireplace. Since the owner of the house hadn't left anything as frivolous as throw pillows, Paul took the cushions off the couch and placed them on the floor near the fire.

"Since we can't move the furniture," he said, "this will have to do." He extended his hand toward her as she stood to one side of the cushions. "Take my hand. I'll help you down. I can't guarantee you'll be more comfortable, but at least you'll be warmer."

"What about you?" She looked at his soaked clothing. "You need to get out of those wet clothes." When he hesitated to answer her, she exclaimed, "You're going back out there, aren't you?"

He had known she wasn't going to like it, but it was something he had to do. "Meredith . . ." he began.

She waved her arm toward the windows. "You're crazy. Take a good look outside. It's getting worse."

The rain hadn't let up at all. If anything, the wind had become stronger, blowing the rain against the windows with incredible force. Occasionally, a spray of sand was thrown up against the glass.

Paul threaded his fingers through her hair. His thumbs soothed and aroused as they stroked the fine line of her jaw.

"On the way back from the store, I drove by the cottage where Nichols and Laura are supposed to be staying. There were lights on in several of the rooms. It was difficult to see through the rain, but I saw two silhouettes on the windows. It could be them. The shades were drawn, but I could tell that one figure was taller than the other."

"If you know they're there, why do you have to go out again?" Meredith asked, annoyed.

"I couldn't be sure the silhouettes were Nichols and your sister. I want to go back and check."

"How do you propose to do that?" Concern for her sister warred with fear for Paul's safety. Anything could happen to him out in that storm. "Dammit, Paul. You could get hurt out there."

She was worried about him, he thought, warm pleasure flowing through him. Not like Tulip fussing over him about not getting enough sleep or eating right. Meredith's eyes reflected her genuine fear. And it was for him.

"Meredith, I'll be all right. It's just a little wind and water."

"That's like saying Noah built an ark to survive a spring shower," she said grumpily. "Under the circumstances, it's an accurate comparison, considering we might be flooded at any time."

He smiled faintly. "The storm will work in my

favor. I can snoop around without them being aware I'm there."

"Why not notify the police? They could check out the house and report back to you here."

"I don't want to involve the North Carolina police. It could get complicated getting him back to Virginia."

"I don't like it."

He took her arm and gently drew her over to the cushions on the floor. Easing her down, he took her crutches and laid them beside her. He was tempted to place them out of her reach in case she got the notion to come after him, but he didn't want her stranded.

He knelt down on one knee and cupped her chin. "I'll be back before you know I'm gone."

His kiss was all too brief, leaving her wanting more. She watched as he straightened and walked toward the door. Before opening it, he looked back at her, then quickly yanked the door open and went out into the driving rain.

Meredith chafed under the forced inactivity, her mind on the man who had just walked out into the storm. If anything happened to him, she didn't know what she was going to do. It wasn't as though she could go find him if he didn't come back. By the time she got out of the driveway, her cast would be soaked, and the crutches would sink into the ground with every step. That was if the wind didn't blow her over first.

Even with all those drawbacks, she knew she would still go after him if he didn't come back soon. She would give him two hours. Then whether he liked it or not, she was going to find him. He hadn't said Nichols was the violent type, but anyone might fight when cornered.

Paul had made no secret of the fact that he badly wanted to find his accountant. That was what had brought them together initially. The thought that haunted her now was whether they would still see each other once Nichols had been found.

Making love wasn't the same as falling in love. Paul could want to do one without wanting the other.

She stared at the fire. He had warned her early on that he wasn't interested in marriage or happily-ever-afters. At the time, she had agreed with him. Now she wanted more than a brief passionate affair, where all they shared was a bed and a search for two thieves.

For the next hour she waited while the storm howled unabated outside. At one point she struggled to her feet to pace in front of the window, imagining all sorts of trouble Paul could find himself in.

The two-hour limit she had set for his return was almost up when she heard the sound of the door latch. Paul had to hold tight to the door so it wouldn't be ripped out of his hands by the wind. Water rolled off him as he stepped inside, spreading a pool around his feet.

"Are you okay?" he asked her, stripping off his shirt.

"I was going to ask you the same thing."

"Other than being wet, I'm fine. Unless the owner has taken the hot water along with everything else, I'm going to take a shower. Then I'll tell you what I found out."

Meredith didn't have any choice but to wait even longer. She was becoming an expert at waiting, she thought wryly. At least she knew he was all right. In order to keep busy, she hobbled into the kitchen and made a couple of sandwiches. A cup of coffee would probably be welcomed, but without electricity, it wasn't possible.

When Paul came out of one of the bedrooms, he immediately looked for Meredith. Startled, he realized it had become a habit to want to see her the moment he entered a room. Seeing her sitting on one of the cushions, the glow from the fire dancing on her hair and skin, he knew it wasn't merely a habit. Being with her was a necessity.

She looked up as he sprawled on the floor next to her, his long legs stretched out toward the fire.

"Feel better?" she asked.

"I forgot what it was like to be dry. I even had sand in my hair."

"I made some sandwiches. They're on the counter."

He shook his head. "I'm not hungry. Maybe later."

His hair was still damp, and she gave in to the temptation to run her fingers through the thick strands. "So tell me what happened."

He shifted her so that she was facing him, resting back against one of his raised legs. "Just getting to the other cottage took longer than I expected. There were objects in the road that weren't supposed to be there, like someone's front gate and a mailbox. Since I didn't have a flashlight and there were no streetlights, it was a challenge not to trip over anything."

She was glad she hadn't known any of that while she was waiting. Cutting right to the meat of the matter, she asked, "Did you see them?"

He grinned at her impatience. "The shades were closed so securely on all the windows, I couldn't see a thing except shadows. I was getting frustrated trying to look in the windows until I decided to make Nichols show himself."

"How did you do that?"

There was a boyish quality to his smile. "I threw a rock at the door."

She laughed. "What happened then?"

"As I expected, Nichols didn't open the door, but he did raise the shade on the window next to the door to look out. From my vantage point across the street, I could see him clearly."

"And my sister?"

He brushed the back of his fingers over her cheek. "I'm sorry, Meredith. I didn't see her. There was a woman with him. I could see that much in the shadows on the shades. Since they supposedly left on the boat together, I think it's safe to assume it was her."

"But you did see Nichols. So what now? Are you going to call the police in Alexandria?"

"Not yet."

She leaned forward as he sat up to toss a couple of small logs into the fire. "What do you mean, not yet? I thought you were so eager to find him and turn him over to the police."

"I didn't say I was going to hand him over to the police. Tray was willing to help me locate him. Besides, if the police go charging in there, your sister would be arrested along with Nichols."

She stared at him. The faint glow from the candles and the wavering golden light from the fire touched his face. His expression was unreadable, though.

"I think," she said slowly, "your nickname needs to be changed. A true rogue wouldn't care about a woman he doesn't know."

He stroked her hair. "It isn't your sister I care

about." His other hand came up to ease her down, until she was resting across his chest. "Don't worry about Laura. I'll get her out of the cottage before I have it out with Nichols."

Her breath caught in her throat as his hands slid over her. She tried desperately not to be disappointed he hadn't said more. He hadn't said he cared about her, just that her sister wasn't the one he cared about. The implication that he did care for her wasn't the same as hearing him declare how he felt. Maybe he never would.

He drew her down beside him, enclosing her securely in his arms. Her lips parted eagerly as his thrusting tongue sought hers.

The storm outside was forgotten as passion swept them into a raging torrent of sensuality. With every touch they hurled themselves toward the ecstasy they found in each other.

Paul drew back as her questing hands found the fastening of his jeans, and she was dimly aware that he was holding himself back to delay the moment when they would come together. It wasn't what she wanted. Not that night. Desperation born of the fear that they would soon part had her clutching, tugging, and stroking him feverishly. Filled with the primitive need to claim him as hers in the only way she knew, she arched her back, pressing herself against him.

She felt an overwhelming satisfaction when he groaned under her passionate assault, his rigid control snapping.

Their clothing was discarded quickly as the tempest churning within them boiled over. She cried out hoarsely when he lifted her over him and filled the emptiness within her.

Their bodies seemed to flow together, moving in

perfect rhythm. She felt her hold on reality start to slip, and clung to him. Unthinkingly, she told him what was in her heart. "I love you."

She was dimly aware of him shuddering against her, but couldn't call the words back. From the depths of her soul, she had meant them. She was also aware he didn't say them back to her.

The last thin threads of sanity ripped apart, hurling them toward the supreme satisfaction awaiting them.

It was odd that even with the aftershocks of pleasure coursing through her, she felt like crying.

The next morning, Paul was oddly distant, which Meredith found hard to understand, especially after the intimacies they had shared during the night. Twice more in the darkness, they had sought each other. She had gone willingly with him into the passionate void of physical fulfillment, her body making the demands she couldn't voice. She didn't repeat her earlier words of love, nor did he make any declaration other than murmuring her name as he slid into her.

His moodiness, she mused, could be because of the lack of sleep, the absence of coffee, or even the hard floor they had slept on. Her gaze went to the window. It couldn't be blamed on the weather. The sun was beginning to rise over the horizon, and the sky was clear.

She went into the bathroom to wash her face and change into clean clothes. Out of the assortment of clothing Tulip had bought for her, she had chosen a fairly conservative white skirt and a black and white striped sweater to bring with her.

While she brushed her hair, she decided to come

right out and ask Paul if something was wrong.
Guessing wasn't doing her any good. It was un-
derstandable if he was preoccupied with Nichols.
But she needed to know it was that and not because she had said she loved him.

She met her troubled gaze in the mirror. A
shaft of pain made her catch her breath as she
admitted he could be reacting to her declaration
of love. Three simple words could be the reason
behind his withdrawal. It was possible love wasn't
what he wanted to hear about, or wanted her to
feel.

Determination straightened her spine. She
wasn't going to take the words back, but she was
going to make him face them.

When she came out of the bathroom, he was
gone.

She went to the door. His car was still there.
That meant he had gone out for a walk on the
beach or to the cottage to confront Nichols and
her sister. Since there wasn't anything she could
do until he returned, she would have to wait.
Again.

She opened the sliding glass door and stepped
out onto the deck. Standing by the rail, she looked
up and down the beach for Paul's tall figure. He
wasn't there.

Several boats were bobbing out on the water
and a few bathers walked along the sand. The
beach bore signs of the storm's savagery, and the
residents next door were collecting plants and lawn
chairs. Apparently they were accustomed to tidy-
ing up after nature's fury.

It was the calm after the storm. Except within
Meredith.

This time she didn't set a time limit for Paul.

He had taken the choice away from her, and she could do nothing except wait to see what happened. Again.

She'd been sitting in a chair on the deck for about thirty minutes when she saw a woman running on the beach. Instead of the normal track suit or even bathing suit, this woman was wearing a nightgown.

Meredith grabbed her crutches and struggled to her feet when she recognized the woman. She was running straight toward the stairs leading up to the house from the beach.

Tears streamed down Laura's pale face when she looked up to see her sister standing on the deck.

"Meredith, you have to do something. That man is going to kill Dan!"

Nine

Laura repeated the same phrase hysterically until she reached the deck and threw herself dramatically onto the faded cushions of the chaise lounge.

Meredith sat back down in her chair and waited for her sister to stop crying. She knew from experience it wouldn't do any good to try to talk to her until Laura had milked the situation to her satisfaction. Laura often used tears to keep from facing the consequences of her own actions.

Meredith had often felt more than two years older than her sister. They were so different, in appearance and personality. Laura was blond and delicate with very little ambition other than looking nice and having a good time.

She finally took one last shuddering breath. Sitting up, she wiped her green eyes with the tips of her fingers. "You have to do something, Merry. A man burst into the cottage and started making all kinds of horrible accusations. He said Dan was a thief and was going to have to pay for what he'd done. He said the police in Virginia were inter-

ested in knowing where he was. Then he ordered
me to come here, saying you were here. What's
going on? Why is he saying all those awful things
about Dan?"

"Because they're true. Dan Nichols stole money
from Paul Rouchett."

"Dan wouldn't do that," Laura said indignantly.

Meredith shook her head. "He did, Laura. Saying
it isn't true doesn't change the truth. He's broken
the law."

"That man is mistaken. Dan doesn't have any
money." A guilty flush tinted her cheeks. "That's
why I needed to borrow money from you so we
could go away together."

"Laura," Meredith said, striving for patience,
"you didn't borrow money from me. You took it.
Without my permission."

"I told you I'd pay you back," she said pouting.

Meredith leaned forward. "Laura, you took all
my money without stopping to think about whether
or not I might need it. This isn't the same as
borrowing my favorite sweater when we were kids.
The money you stole from me just so you could
take a thief on a vacation was to pay my rent and
buy my food until I could get back to work. Taking my money was just as wrong as Nichols stealing from his employer."

Laura had the grace to look ashamed. "I didn't
realize you needed it or I wouldn't have taken it."

Meredith sighed heavily. "Yes, you would." Deciding to give her sister a scare, she added, "Paul
Rouchett reported Nichols's theft to the police. He
has a friend on the force who's been looking for
your boyfriend. Maybe I should have done the
same thing."

"Meredith! I'm your sister."

"And that is supposed to entitle you to steal from me? You think just because we have the same parents and were raised together that gives you the right to whatever I have?" Realizing she was wasting her breath, she stopped. "Do you have any of the money left, Laura? Or is it all gone?"

Laura fussed with the skirt of her filmy nightgown. "I don't know. I gave it to Dan."

Meredith bid her money a mental farewell. Reaching for her crutches, she levered herself out of the chair. "Come inside. You'll have to wear the clothes I wore yesterday, but at least you'll be decently covered."

Surprisingly, Laura didn't argue, but followed her sister into the cottage. "Are the police going to be coming here?"

"I don't know what Paul plans to do. I think he wants to take Dan back to Virginia rather than turn him over to the North Carolina police."

Laura started crying again. "This is all so awful."

Meredith couldn't have agreed more. She took the leather skirt and oversize white sweater from the suitcase and held them out to Laura. "Breaking the law is awful."

"No, I mean the way that man burst into the cottage this morning."

Meredith saw her sister's eyes widen in horror as she accepted the skirt and sweater. She thought it was because of the clothes until Laura said, "You don't think he's going to hurt Dan, do you?"

"It's a possibility."

•   •   •

Paul didn't return to the cottage until an hour later, and he wasn't alone. The man with him wasn't at all what Meredith had expected an accountant to look like, especially a crooked accountant. If there was a contest for the most all-American, squeaky-clean-looking man, Dan Nichols would win.

Provided his hands weren't tied behind his back.

Aside from the initial hysterical outburst from Laura, there were no further scenes. The fact that Paul had everything under complete control didn't surprise Meredith. After arranging her life, Mr. Bowers's, her dog's, a cleaning crew, plus managing his club, one thief must have been small potatoes.

Whatever had happened at the cottage between the two men wasn't discussed. Paul said very little other than they would be driving back to Alexandria immediately.

It was a strange ride. For once Laura was silent and subdued as she sat beside Meredith in the backseat. In the front seat Nichols protested once about how uncomfortable he was with his hands tied, but a stony glance from Paul shut him up.

Meredith had an idea what was going through her sister's mind, even Dan Nichols's mind. They were both worried about the consequences of their actions. She certainly knew what she herself was thinking. What was going to happen between her and Paul now that they had found his accountant and her sister?

What she didn't know was what Paul was thinking.

When they arrived at the hotel, he parked at the front entrance. He helped Meredith out of the backseat, then took their suitcase from the trunk. Handing it to Ralph, he instructed the doorman to make sure Meredith got into the hotel safely.

Laura opened her door to get out, too, but Paul ordered her to stay in the car. She gave him a scorching look, yet shut the door just the same. Meredith grabbed Paul's arm as he turned to get back into the car.

"Wait a minute. Where are you going?"

"I'll be back in a little while."

"That's no answer."

"I don't have time for explanations now, Meredith. Go with Ralph."

She couldn't believe it. He was leaving her and driving away with Laura and Nichols. She had no idea where they were going or why. All she knew was that she wasn't included.

Ralph was waiting patiently for her to follow the instructions Rogue had given. Anger stirred. It was about time she took control of her own life again.

She entered the hotel but didn't go up to Paul's apartment. She was no longer going along with what he told her.

Tulip wasn't in her office, but Baxter was in his. He knew the answer to Meredith's first question. "Your apartment has been thoroughly cleaned, Miss Claryon. The carpets and the drapes have been removed. The drapes will be cleaned, but the carpet will have to be replaced. The odor should dissipate in a couple of days."

She didn't have to ask who was paying for the cleaning expenses. Her debts were growing. "When will I be able to return to my apartment?"

"Anytime you want. There wasn't as much smoke

damage done in your place as there was in Mr. Bowers's. I took him back yesterday so he could get started on cleaning his trains."

"I'll be going home too, Baxter. If you'll tell me Tulip's address, I'll pick up my dog and take him with me."

Baxter frowned. "Rogue didn't say anything about you going home yet, Miss Claryon."

"He's had other things on his mind." She met Baxter's gaze squarely. "I hate to ask, but I can't drive because of my cast. Could you arrange for a car to take me to Tulip's, then home?"

He looked uncomfortable. "I don't know, Miss Claryon. I really should check with Rogue first. He might have other plans."

He undoubtedly did, she thought. "If you won't make the arrangements, I'll call a taxi."

Obviously against his better judgment, Baxter agreed to get her a car, although he said he would have to check with Tulip first about the dog. Apparently, he wasn't about to oppose both Rogue and Tulip.

An hour later Meredith was in her apartment. The cleaning crew had worked miracles in such a short time. The walls and woodwork were clean and had even been repainted. The appliances in the kitchen sparkled, as did the bathroom fixtures. She guessed her clothes had been washed, too, for they smelled fresh and clean. Only a faint smoky odor hung in the air like bad incense, and she could live with that.

Sitting down in her chair, she reached for the phone and punched out a number. She was switching from the backseat to the driver's seat for a change.

•   •   •

It took the rest of the day and half of the night for Paul to tie up the loose ends with the police. They weren't too happy that he wasn't going to press charges against Dan Nichols. Tray went along with Paul, though he put a scare into Nichols, telling him what would happen if he didn't come up with the money he had taken. Nichols gave them the numbers of the three different accounts he had deposited the money in, swearing he hadn't spent any of it. Assured of getting his money back, Paul decided there was nothing to be gained by having Nichols arrested. Maybe a week ago he would have wanted every ounce of justice meted out to the man. Now he was content just to have the money returned.

He felt as though a heavy weight had been lifted off his shoulders as he entered the hotel. Now that the situation with Nichols was out of the way, he could concentrate on something more important. His relationship with Meredith.

Ralph was no longer on duty, and Tulip had also gone home. The lobby was fairly quiet, although he could hear the faint sounds of merriment coming from The Rogue's Den. It was the last place he wanted to be right then. He wanted to see Meredith. He wanted to see the relief in her eyes when he told her how he had resolved the situation with Nichols and her sister.

One thing he wasn't going to mention was the conversation he had with her sister. When Nichols struck the deal to return all the money so Paul would let him off the hook with the police, Paul realized Laura had financed their travels—with Meredith's money. He found out from Laura how much she had taken, learning she had left her sister practically destitute.

In his pocket he had the exact amount to give to Meredith. He knew her well enough to realize she wouldn't take it if she thought it was from him. He was going to imply he had gotten it from her sister. Hopefully, it was the only white lie he would ever have to tell her.

When he opened the door of his apartment and found the living room dark, he wasn't surprised. He also wasn't disappointed. The thought of Meredith asleep in his bed had been the reason he had hurried back to the hotel.

He began unbuttoning his shirt as he strode toward his bedroom. Pushing open the door, he stepped inside and slowly walked over to the bed. As his eyes adjusted to the dark and he was able to see clearly, he stopped. It was empty.

Turning on the bedside lamp, he stared down at the smooth spread for a few seconds, then sank down onto the bed. Where in hell was she, he wondered, fear coiling tightly in his stomach. This wasn't the way he had planned the evening to end.

He remembered the confused expression on her face when he had left her in front of the hotel. He had seen the bewildered hurt in her eyes, but he hadn't taken the time to tell her what he was doing. He had wanted to keep her out of it.

Evidently, she had felt left out.

Reaching for the phone, he jabbed out the number for her apartment. His fingers tapped impatiently on the bedside table while he waited for her to answer. After three rings he heard her voice, but it was her answering machine.

He felt like throwing the phone across the room. Dammit, where was she at eleven o'clock at night?

He had a sudden thought. Punching out the number for the club downstairs, he waited for Baxter to answer.

When he did, Paul barked, "Is Meredith in the club?"

"She went back to her own apartment, Rogue," Baxter replied cautiously.

"Why?" Paul's voice was dangerously quiet.

There was an audible gulp on the line. "She didn't say. She came into the office earlier today and asked how far the cleaning crew had gotten with her apartment. I told her they were through. She asked me to arrange for a ride for her so she could pick up her dog and go home. I told her I had to ask Tulip first, but she said she would deal with Tulip when she got there."

"Are you sure she went home? She doesn't answer her phone."

"I drove her there myself. She doesn't have the dog. Tulip wasn't around, so we couldn't get Ivan. I saw Meredith safely up the stairs, and as far as I know, she's still there."

"Okay. Thanks, Baxter."

"Ah, Rogue," the other man began hesitantly, as though testing the waters before jumping in. "I hope I did the right thing. I told her she should wait until you got back, but she was adamant."

"You did fine, Baxter. I appreciate your seeing her home personally. She would have found a way to get there on her own if you hadn't taken care of it."

Baxter laughed. "She did threaten to call a taxi. She seemed pretty determined."

That was obvious, Paul thought, saying goodbye to Baxter. But determined about what? And why now? He fell back onto the bed and stared at the ceiling. If she was determined to put him out of her life, she was in for a very big surprise.

He tried her apartment again. When he got the machine, he left a message for her to call him no matter what the time.

Knowing he couldn't simply wait for her to call, he sprang off the bed and began undressing. A quick shower, a change of clothes, and he was going to her apartment. If she wasn't there, he was damn well going to find her.

This time when he climbed the stairs and stood in front of her door, he didn't kick it in. He felt like it, but he didn't. The first knock was normal, a light series of taps. After what he considered a decent waiting period, he knocked again. A little harder. When she still didn't come to the door, he pounded.

"Meredith, I know you're in there. Mr. Bowers said he heard your crutches through his ceiling and I can see a light under the door."

He heard a faint sound but couldn't make out what she said. "I can't hear you. Open the door, Meredith."

"It's not locked!" she yelled.

That information should have made him happy, since he could get into her apartment without breaking down the door—again—but it also meant she had left herself unprotected—again. Hearing her voice also meant she was all right. The fear in his stomach began to uncurl.

He yanked open the door and entered, prepared to comment on her carelessness. She was seated in the same chair as before with her foot propped up on the hassock. No, not quite like before. There was no cast on her leg.

Closing the door, he leaned against it. "I thought you weren't due to have the cast removed until next week."

"I wasn't."

As though unsure of his footing, he slowly walked over to her, stopping inches away. Her leg looked odd without the cast. Even with an elastic bandage wrapped around it, her ankle was slim and shapely.

"What made you decide to have the cast taken off now?"

"It felt ready."

He stepped around the hassock and sat down on the couch. Something on the floor between her chair and the hassock caught his attention. It was an ice pack.

"Was it ready?" he asked, bringing his gaze back to her.

She shrugged. "Enough to have the cast removed."

She could have added that the orthopedic doctor on duty at the hospital had tried to talk her out of it. To be exact, Buddy O'Neil told her she was nuts. Only after he saw the Xrays that showed the break had healed did he agree to let her go without the cast. She had still needed the crutches to get up the stairs after one of the nurses had dropped her off thirty minutes earlier.

"What's your hurry?" Paul asked. "Were you that eager to get rid of the Rogue's logo I'd drawn on your cast?"

She didn't answer his question but asked one of her own. "What happened with Nichols and Laura?"

Sitting back, he let his head rest on the couch. "Nichols and I made a deal. If he gave me back the money, he didn't have to go to jail."

She didn't try to hide her surprise. "You're being kind of easy on him, aren't you? I got the impression you wouldn't be satisfied with less than his head on a platter."

His dark eyes drilled into her. "I discovered there were more important things than retaliation. I settled for my money and Nichols got his freedom. He's without a job and doesn't expect a reference from me when he tries to get another one."

"What about Laura?"

"Are you sure she's your sister?" he asked bluntly. "I've never met two women more unlike each other than you and her." As though to prove a point, he added, "She dropped Nichols like a hot penny when she found out he was a thief." He reached into his pocket and took out a folded bundle of money held together with a money clip. "Here is the money your sister took from you," he said, tossing it onto her lap.

Astonished, she picked up the money. "I can't believe she still had it. She told me she'd given it to Nichols, and I thought for sure it would have all been spent."

Paul didn't want to delve too deeply into the subject of the money. The less he had to lie to her, the better it would be for both of them. "She seemed suitably chastened when I dropped her off at her apartment. I imagine she'll be getting in touch with you soon."

Meredith placed the money on the table next to her. A week ago getting it back had been the most important thing. Now it took second place to what she was going to have to do.

Paul was puzzled by her preoccupied expression. He had expected her to be happy to have her savings returned. "What's going on, Meredith? Why did you come back here instead of waiting for me at the hotel?"

They were perfectly normal questions for him to ask under the circumstances, she mused, but difficult for her to answer. She met his intent gaze with effort. "As a nurse, I've had occasion to witness patients' reactions when they discover they have an incurable disease. Some want to end it all right then rather than wait for nature to take its inevitable course. Some deny it and won't face it. Others decide to pack in as much as they can into every hour of every day. No matter which way people react, the knowledge that they have an incurable malady changes their life, requiring them to make adjustments, some major and some minor."

He sat up straight. "Meredith, are you ill? Did they find something wrong when they took the Xrays?"

"It's not physical."

"Meredith, you're scaring me. What are you talking about?"

She had gone this far, she told herself. Taking a deep breath, she gazed directly at him. "I'm in love with you, and I want to marry you."

Stunned, Paul stared at her. He not only had trouble thinking, breathing wasn't all that easy either. When his mind began to kick in, he started to rise, but Meredith held up her hand to stop him.

"Wait. I'm not through." He sat back down, his gaze never wavering from her face. "I've done a lot of thinking since you left me at the hotel earlier. Everything between us has happened very quickly and started because we were searching for your accountant and my sister. Our time together has been because of unusual circumstances. The smoke damage to my apartment, sleeping in your bed, your buying me clothes, and the trip to North Carolina. You've run the whole show, and I let you, but not any longer. Now that you've found Nichols, the reason for us to be together no longer exists. There has to be more."

"The original reason might not exist any longer, but we are going to continue to see each other."

That wasn't precisely what she'd been hoping to hear. "As what?"

He got to his feet and started pacing back and forth. "What do you mean, as what? Dammit, Meredith, you aren't making any sense. One minute you tell me you love me, then you tell me . . . Hell, I don't know what you're trying to tell me."

He couldn't even say the word *marriage*, she thought. She could understand his confusion too. Her explanation was as clear as a muddy pond. Somehow, she had to make him understand. She couldn't back down now. It was too important. "If we do continue seeing each other, it has to be under different rules, because the other one doesn't apply now that you've found Nichols. I have become involved with you, and I would like it to be permanent. If you can't accept that, then we should stop seeing each other."

If a bomb had gone off in the room, he couldn't have looked more shocked. He stopped pacing and stared down at her. "I don't like ultimatums, Meredith."

"I'm not crazy about giving them."

"You're serious, aren't you?"

She nodded, unable to speak because of the tightness in her throat. So much depended on his answer, and she had the sinking feeling it wasn't going to be the one she wanted to hear.

Feeling as though a trap were about to clamp around him, Paul took an instinctive step away from her. "I've been honest with you, Meredith. I'm not interested in marriage."

"Okay," she said, struggling not to let her disappointment show.

He placed his hands on his hips and frowned. "What's okay?"

"I wanted to know where you stood and now I know. I think you should leave. I'm starting physical therapy early tomorrow morning, and I'd like to get to bed."

The trap had closed, but he hadn't been caught in it. He had been shut out instead. Dropping his hands, he walked to the door. "Are you sure this is the way you want it?"

Her heart was shredding, but she managed to meet his dark gaze. "Yes."

With one last glance, he left.

Meredith stared at the closed door, wrapping her arms around her middle to hold in the pain. Knowing she had lost Paul hurt more than anything she had ever experienced before. When she had decided to confront him, she'd known there was a fifty-fifty chance he would do exactly what he'd done.

A tear escaped the corner of her eye and rolled slowly down her cheek. She might have expected it, but she wasn't ready for it. Nor had she thought it was going to hurt so much.

• • •

By eleven o'clock the following morning Meredith felt as though she had put in a double shift at the hospital. Her ankle was throbbing and painful after two hours of physical therapy. She didn't need the therapist to tell her she was rushing the therapy so soon after the cast had been removed. It was vitally important for her to stand on her own two feet, literally and figuratively.

She had been forced to trade the crutches for a cane, since her ankle was still weak. She had hoped to do without either, but she had to admit she needed some support.

Still unable to drive, she had to take a taxi back to her apartment. The driver opened the door for her and assisted her to her feet. After paying him, she crossed the grass verge to the sidewalk.

No matter how hard she tried, she couldn't walk without limping. It was the first thing Paul noticed as she came around the corner of the house.

Meredith halted suddenly when she saw him sitting on the steps to her apartment. Her heart stopped for an instant, then started beating painfully hard.

"What are you doing here, Paul?"

"I would think that was obvious. I'm waiting for you."

She stared at him. He sounded as tired as he looked. His shirt was slightly rumpled, as though he had slept in his clothes. His long, jean-clad legs were stretched out over the two steps below him, one ankle crossed over the other.

"I told you last night I had physical therapy this morning."

His gaze moved from her face to the cane,

then to her foot. "Do you want help going up the stairs?"

She shook her head, feeling panic. She was barely hanging on to her control just looking at him. She would never be able to handle being in his arms.

Levering his long legs under him, he stood up, blocking her way as she took a step forward. "Are you going to ask me in?"

"What's the point, Paul?" she said wearily. "I haven't changed my mind since last night."

"I have."

Her eyes widened in shock. Hope made a valiant attempt to rise within her. But common sense also filtered through the hope. If he was proposing marriage, he didn't appear very happy about it.

Her fingers tightened around the cane. "What exactly are you saying?"

"I want you to live with me."

Hope dwindled, falling as though made of frail matchsticks. Living together would be a way for them to be with each other, but it wasn't the commitment she wanted. "It wouldn't work, Paul. I want more than a temporary relationship. I couldn't just live with you. It goes against everything I believe in. In some ways I'm a woman of the ninetie's, but down deep I'm still back in the fifties, when silly things like fidelity and commitment were the norm rather than the exception."

Frustration tightened his mouth. "I would be committed to you in every way except legally, Meredith. Isn't that enough?"

The small word was hard to say. Possibly the most difficult word she had ever had to pronounce. "No."

He slammed a fist down onto the railing. "Dammit, what do you want from me? I'm willing to give you everything: a place by my side, in my bed and my life. I'd be faithful. There would be no one else but you. I would expect the same promise from you. The only time limit I'm putting on our relationship is a lifetime. If you don't like the idea of living in a hotel, we could find somewhere else where you would be more comfortable."

He still didn't get it, she thought. She would live in a hut with him under the right circumstances. The where didn't matter. The how did. He might be against marriage, but it was the only commitment that would justify their relationship.

She couldn't take much more, having him so close that she could reach out and touch him, yet so far away from her in every way that was important.

"We don't want the same things," she said. Her voice trembled no matter how she tried to control it. "Let's just leave it at that."

"Hold on to the cane." In one easy motion he lifted her off her feet and carried her up the stairs. After setting her down, he held on to her arms and lowered his head. He kissed her hard, hunger and desperation mixed with passion.

"I'm not going to lose you, Meredith," he said against her lips. "We have more between us than most people find in two lifetimes. A piece of paper won't change that."

His fingers tightened on her arms, just short of causing her pain. He covered her mouth again, then released her abruptly. Turning away from her, he strode down the steps, two at a time. At the bottom he stopped and looked up at her.

"You know where to find me if you change your mind."

Numb with pain, she watched as he disappeared around the corner of the house, then fumbled with her keys to unlock the door. Once inside, she sank down onto the chair. Ivan came over to her, somehow realizing she needed comfort and companionship, not demands.

She reached out and stroked his head, then buried her face into his fur as she let the tears she had held back finally fall.

Ten

Paul was sitting behind his desk in his darkened office. Downstairs in the club the music was loud, every table was occupied, and the cash register was continually ringing. Lovers were gazing into each other's eyes and couples were dancing closely on the small dance floor. Laughter and chatter competed with the music as everyone enjoyed an evening at The Rogue's Den. His money was sitting in his bank account, where it belonged.

He should be happy. He wasn't.

His tuxedo jacket was crumpled up on a chair, along with his black tie. He didn't plan on putting either on again, even though it was only nine o'clock in the evening.

The neck of a bottle rang against a crystal glass as he poured several fingers of Scotch. Lifting the glass, he brought it to his lips and drank.

"I thought you hated the taste of booze."

He should have locked the door, he thought, cursing silently. The last thing he wanted was company. "You forgot to knock, Tulip."

She flicked the wall switch and light flooded the room. Paul squinted against the sudden brightness, then scowled. Undaunted, Tulip walked over to the desk.

"And you forgot you promised the Warings to join them for an anniversary toast."

"Stand in for me. I'm not in the mood for toasting true love."

"I've been standing in for you for two weeks, Rogue. This has to stop. Either sell the club or go after her."

He slammed the glass down onto the desktop. "That's enough, Tulip. Butt out."

"No, I won't. Everyone's been walking on tiptoe around you, and I'm tired of making excuses for why you aren't in the club. You have to do something about Meredith or forget her."

Forget Meredith, he thought. That was like saying forget breathing. He couldn't manage to do without either one. And he had tried to forget her. Lord knows he had tried.

"I need the club. It pays the bills."

Tulip's expression softened. She came around the desk and put her hand on his shoulder. "Rogue, you need her too. Why don't you at least go talk to her? Whatever problem you two have can be worked out, but not if you don't see her."

"It's not that simple. She's not satisfied with the way things were, and I was. She wants something more permanent."

"It's not exactly an unusual request," Tulip said dryly. "Of course, some women don't mind being an occasional roll in the hay." She saw the spark of temper in his eyes and smiled that her darts had hit their target.

"That's not the way it was with Meredith, and you know it," he said angrily.

"I know it. I just wanted to see if you did. Some women are mistress material, Rogue. Meredith isn't."

"And I'm not marriage material. I've tried it twice, remember?"

"Fine. Have it your way. I can see you're quite happy like this. If it's any consolation, Meredith wasn't exactly jumping for joy when she came to pick up Ivan."

"It's no consolation." He didn't want Meredith to be unhappy. That was part of the reason he wouldn't tie her down to marriage with him.

"You're probably doing the right thing," Tulip went on, twisting the knife. "Don't take another chance up to bat when you've had two strikes against you. You could strike again and be out." She headed for the door. "Or you could hit a home run. Emphasis on home."

Paul laid his head back and closed his eyes after she left. He really didn't need Tulip to tell him he'd been a fool. He already knew that. Everywhere he looked in his apartment, he saw reminders of Meredith. He couldn't take a shower without thinking of the water and soap caressing her skin. Sleeping in the bed where they had made love was pure torture. Eating in his dining room was also out. She was everywhere, even though she wasn't there.

Going to his studio hadn't worked either. She was there too.

And deeply imbedded in his heart.

Suddenly he sprang from his chair and rushed out of the room as though something were chasing him. But he couldn't run away from himself.

• • •

Meredith's ankle was throbbing, yet she ignored it. She smiled down at the child who was getting stitches in his arm to close a three-inch gash.

"You're doing fine, Tommy," she said gently, brushing away a tear from the corner of the child's eye. "Dr. Blackstone has the fastest needle in the east. When he's through, we'll count the stitches, then you'll be able to tell all your friends how many you have in your arm."

"Travis had eight stitches in his head last summer."

Her smile widened. "You have a lot more stitches than Travis. You be sure and tell him so." She took a strip of tape she'd decorated with different colored felt pens and stuck it on his shirt. "You can also show him the medal you received for bravery."

Dr. Blackstone tied off the last stitch. "As soon as Nurse Claryon puts a bandage on your cut, you can go home. Try to stay away from broken glass from now on. Okay?"

Tommy nodded and watched as Meredith wrapped gauze around his forearm. When she was finished, she summoned Tommy's mother. Her ankle almost gave out when she stepped aside to let an orderly pushing a patient in a wheelchair pass. She recovered her balance by placing her hand on the wall. Unfortunately, she was seen.

Dr. Buddy O'Neil came up behind her and put his arm around her waist. "Lean on me."

"I'm fine. Just give me a minute."

He ignored her protests. "You're taking more than a minute. You're going home after you put an ice pack on that ankle."

"I can't go home. I have another two hours on my shift."

"Your second shift today. What are you trying to do, Meredith? Destroy all my good work?" He barked out an order to one of the other nurses to bring an ice pack to the nurses' lounge.

Once Meredith was seated, he pulled a stool over in front of her and lifted her foot to unwind the elastic bandage. His sharp gaze noted the shadows under her eyes her makeup hadn't managed to conceal. "Or are you trying to work yourself into the ground for other reasons?"

"I'm a dedicated nurse," she said lightly. "Didn't you know that?"

She might have been joking, but he wasn't. "I know you are, Meredith, and you're a good nurse, which is why you should know better than to rush an injury."

"I have the next two days off," she said as he rewrapped her ankle after examining it. "I promise to rest my ankle."

He shook his head. "You're taking the next week off. There's no use glaring at me like that, Meredith. You're ankle is swollen more than it should be, and you know it. You either go voluntarily or I throw my weight around."

Meredith blinked. He was serious. The nurses rarely heard that tone from Dr. O'Neil. He was generally one of the most easygoing doctors on the staff.

"All right," she agreed. "I'll take a week off, although it will be without pay and under protest."

"How long have we known each other, Meredith? A year? Year and a half?"

"A little over a year. Why?"

"I remember when we had a slow night last

winter, you listened to my sad tale of woe about breaking up with Rachel. You didn't give advice or preach. You listened. I'd be happy to do the same for you anytime you need to talk about that man."

"What man?"

"The one who's the reason you've reported back to work before you should and taken double shifts so you don't have time to think about him."

Was she that transparent, she wondered. "It didn't work out. He went his way, and I went mine."

"Is he happier about it than you are?"

She shrugged. "I imagine he's surviving. Rogues usually land on their feet."

The nurse who brought in the ice pack also brought in a request for Dr. O'Neil to see a patient who'd just come in. Giving Meredith the ice pack, she added, "The woman who brought this guy in asked for you, Meredith. She wanted to know if you were on duty." She chuckled. "She had an unusual name. Tulip."

The ice bag fell off Meredith's ankle when she sat up abruptly. "Did you say Tulip? Whom did she bring in?"

"A gorgeous man she called Rogue. If he is, I'm going to change my mind about rogues."

"What's wrong with him?" Meredith asked anxiously.

"He broke his ankle."

When she checked, Meredith learned Paul had been taken to X-ray, so she went to the waiting room to talk to Tulip. She was leafing through a magazine. She smiled when she saw Meredith. "Hello, dear. How nice to see you again."

"What happened to Paul?" Meredith asked, sitting down in the chair beside her.

"The light in the stairwell leading up to his studio was out, and he tripped. He fell down only a couple of stairs, but he's done something to his ankle."

"When did this happen?"

"Sometime during the night." She gave Meredith a strange look. "He hasn't been sleeping too well and spends a lot of time in his studio. Luckily, I was worried about him and had decided to take him something to eat. At first I thought he had fallen down the stairs because he'd been drinking, but . . ."

"Paul doesn't drink."

"He has been lately." She placed a hand on Meredith's. "He misses you."

"He's known where to find me."

"Pride can be a powerful deterrent, especially for a man. He does need you, Meredith."

"Not enough, Tulip. I've worked too hard for my self-respect to throw it away on a part-time relationship. He doesn't want marriage, and I don't want less. That doesn't leave a lot of room for negotiation."

"How about compromise? It seems to me something can be worked out if two people care enough."

"I don't know what Paul's feelings are."

"Why not ask him?"

She made it sound so easy, Meredith mused. "I'll go see how he's doing."

She found him sitting on the table in one of the treatment rooms, having a cast put on his left ankle. He was wearing the denim shirt from the loft. One leg of his jeans had been cut off above the knee so he would be able to remove them over the cast. She saw shock enter his eyes when she walked into the room. She also saw pain.

Sitting on a stool in front of a pull-down shelf, Dr. O'Neil was writing up the patient's report. He looked up when Meredith entered.

"Claryon, I told you to stay off that foot."

"I know this patient. How bad is the break?" She glanced over his shoulder to see what he had written. "A compound fracture."

Dr. O'Neil grinned as he glanced from Meredith to the patient, who hadn't taken his eyes off her since she walked into the room. "According to all those large medical books I studied, broken bones aren't contagious. You and your friend seem to be exceedingly clumsy."

She walked over to Paul and placed her hand on his thigh. "What happened?"

"Move your hand, green eyes," he murmured. "My foot hurts like hell. I don't need another ache."

Dr. O'Neil choked, then started coughing. When he could speak, he turned to the technician who had finished the cast and was washing his hands. "I think we'd better leave Nurse Claryon to handle this one, Charley." He laughed. "He'll be in good hands."

As he passed Meredith, Dr. O'Neil handed her a prescription form. "This is for pain. Fill him in on the rest. I left a treatment sheet on the desk."

"Is he going to need to stay overnight?"

The doctor glanced at Paul. "I suggested it. He refused."

"I'm not staying in the hospital," Paul said crossly.

Dr. O'Neil grinned at Meredith. "It's a good thing

we aren't sensitive here. No one ever wants to stay." Becoming serious, he added, "He should have someone with him for a few days until he gets used to the crutches. Maybe he'll listen to you since you've gone through it yourself."

"Yes, Doctor," she answered automatically, her gaze remaining on Paul.

"And try to relax," the doctor went on, "and get some rest during your time off, Meredith. We need you around here to take care of patients, not be one."

"Yes, Doctor," she repeated, smiling faintly.

After the door closed, Meredith stepped over to the stool Buddy had used. She began reading the instructions from the treatment sheet, her voice professionally cool as she told him about warning signs and not getting the cast wet.

Paul was hungry for the sight of her and devoured her with his eyes. She appeared thinner in her white uniform, and there were dark circles under her eyes. When she had entered the room, he had also noticed how she favored her right foot. He loved the sound of her voice, although he wasn't listening to what she was saying.

When she paused for a breath, he spoke her name. "Come here."

Dropping the sheet, she sprang off the stool and rushed over to him. "What's wrong? Are you in pain?"

He took her hand and pulled her closer. "Yes. I've been in pain since I left you that last time."

"It was your choice."

"I know. It was a lousy choice." He started to turn sideways, but he had forgotten about the cast. Wincing in pain, he muttered under his breath.

"Your cast isn't dry yet. You have to stay there for a little while longer."

He held her with his eyes since he wasn't able to hold her any other way. "How long do I have to wait?"

She glanced at her watch. "Another ten minutes or so should do it. Then you can go home. You know Dr. O'Neil was right when he said you should have someone stay with you for a few days. You're going to have some pain and some adjustments to make. Just getting around on the crutches will take practice."

"It sounds like I could use a nurse."

She turned away. She wasn't going to be able to take much more of this. Seeing him, hearing his voice, hurt too much. So was being away from him.

"There's a nurse registry you can call. They can send someone out."

"I would rather have someone I know. I heard the doctor say you were taking some time off. I'd like—"

She didn't let him finish. Whirling around, she said angrily, "Stop it! What are you doing, Paul? I'm not something you can pick up and put down whenever it suits your mood."

"Meredith—"

"I meant what I said. I can't be what you want. I love you, dammit. That means I want to spend the rest of my life with you. It doesn't entitle you to play with my feelings like this. You've made your own feelings just as clear as I have. You want me physically but not emotionally. Fine, I've accepted that. Eventually, I'll even be able to live with it, but not if you keep playing with me like this."

"I'm not playing," he said quietly.

"What do you call wanting me to be your nurse? Do you really think I can be with you, touch you, hear your voice, and not be torn apart when you no longer need my services either as a nurse or as a woman?" She heard the almost hysterical ring in her voice and took a deep breath before she went on. "Down deep inside I'm still that naive farm girl from Nebraska who expects such odd things as old-fashioned courtship and promises of forever. You don't." She shoved the treatment sheet and his prescription into his hand. "I'm not for hire."

She heard him calling her name as she left the room. It was unfair for her to run out on him when he couldn't possibly come after her. She didn't feel fair, though. She felt like kicking something.

The flowers started arriving the next morning. First there were a dozen white roses delivered by a woman dressed in a tuxedo. The card had no signature, only a drawing of a man wearing a red bandanna and a patch over one eye. The Rogue.

An hour later a man wearing bright green pants with a matching vest and bow tie handed her a bouquet of four-leaf clovers. Again the Rogue appeared on the card.

In the afternoon a plump woman with bunny ears and a plush pink costume complete with a large pom-pom for a tail appeared at the door with a handful of balloons. They were handed over with a card. Meredith didn't have to look at the card to know whom the balloons were from.

That evening she sat in her living room staring

at the roses for a long time. Hope was beginning to grow where only loneliness and despair had taken root. But her phone remained silent.

The next morning after returning from taking Ivan out for a walk, she was greeted at her door by a menagerie of stuffed animals all wearing black eye patches. It took four trips to get them all into her apartment with Ivan carrying one bright yellow giraffe in his mouth.

After a five-pound box of expensive chocolates was delivered, Meredith picked up the telephone. She tried Paul's private number, but only got his answering machine. She left her name and asked him to call her.

The rest of the day she kept waiting either for him to phone or for the next delivery. Ivan had a very brief walk so she could return home quickly. Nothing happened. The telephone didn't ring, and there were no more strangely dressed people knocking on her door.

The hope that had budded within her began to wilt.

While she was fixing her lunch the next day, there was a loud rap on her door. Dropping the knife onto the counter, she rushed to the door and threw it open. A husky man with a fat cigar stuck in his mouth was standing there. He was dressed in tan coveralls with a patch over one pocket advertising a well-known electronics store.

"You Meredith Claryon?" he asked in a rough, gravely voice.

"Yes."

He gestured to someone down the stairs. "Bring it up, Harvey."

Meredith had to duck back out of the way when the first man stepped across the threshold. He stopped abruptly when he saw Ivan sitting several feet away.

"Does he bite?"

"Only if I tell him to," she said as a warning.

The man named Harvey was half the other man's size, yet apparently was the one assigned to tote a stack of boxes up the stairs. "Where do you want these, lady?"

"I don't know. What is it?"

The bigger man read off the clipboard he held in one hand. "One CD player, two speakers, and a package of disks."

In an astonishingly short amount of time, Harvey had everything hooked up while the man with the clipboard supervised. One of the CDs was popped into the player to test it, and a soft, romantic ballad filled her living room. After she signed an invoice, she was handed a book of instructions and the two men left.

She sank down in her chair as the music swirled around the room, gazing at the card stapled to the cover of the instruction book. Beneath the rogue logo, Paul had written, "Dancing is part of courtship, but under the circumstances all I can provide is the music."

She punched out Paul's phone number again. After listening to the recording of his voice, she was about to leave another message when someone knocked at her door.

Wondering what next, she opened the door. When she saw a delivery man standing there, she simply held out her hand to take the square box from him.

Back in her chair, she lifted the gaily wrapped lid and took out a glass-enclosed music box. It had a ceramic base with two figures on it, a man and a woman dressed in formal clothes and in each other's arms. Looking closely, Meredith saw a tiny white bandage around the man's left foot. She depressed the lever, and the dancers began to whirl to the tune of a tinkling waltz.

She turned off the music box and set it on the table, moving aside one of the stuffed animals to make room. Her gaze took in all the gifts she had received.

This wasn't courtship. It was an out-and-out assault.

She got his recording again when she called once more. She couldn't understand why he wasn't answering the phone. He didn't come himself but sent gifts to show he was thinking of her. It could be the start of a different relationship between them.

But not if she couldn't talk to him.

Giving up on phoning his apartment, she dialed the other number on his card, the nightclub. When Baxter answered, she asked to speak to Tulip.

"She's not here right now. Can I take a message?"

"This is Meredith Claryon. Do you know when she'll be back?"

His tone changed from business to pleasure. "I'm not sure when she'll be back, Meredith. She's taking care of Rogue. Did you know he broke his ankle?"

"Yes, I know about his ankle. Is he in his apartment or in the loft?"

"His apartment."

"Thanks, Baxter."

After hanging up, she hurried into her bedroom and flung off her jeans and sweater, leaving them where they fell.

If he couldn't come to her, she would go to him. It was either that, or she was going to have to move into a bigger apartment.

Tulip answered the door. Her face lit up with joy when she saw Meredith. Opening the door wider, she said, "Well, it's about time. Now maybe Rogue will stop pacing the floor."

"Pacing the floor? With a broken ankle?"

Tulip gestured for her to come in. "It was a figure of speech."

Meredith smiled faintly. "He's not a very good patient?"

"Patience is the operative word. Now that you're here, I'll go catch up on things I've been neglecting the last couple of days. He's in his bedroom."

"No, I'm not."

Both women looked in the direction of the man's voice.

He was standing at the other end of the living room, leaning on crutches and wearing only a pair of cutoff jeans and a shirt open down the front. The white cast was stark against his tanned leg.

Neither noticed when Tulip let herself quietly out of the apartment.

Meredith tore her gaze away from his to glance at his cast. "You're managing better than I did at first."

He didn't want to talk about his injury. "I was wondering if you were ever going to come."

She walked slowly toward him. "You never called me back. I wanted to thank you for sending the flowers and all the rest. Didn't you get my message?"

He had played the tape over and over just to

hear her voice. "I didn't want to talk to you on the phone. I needed you here in person."

"I'm here."

His mouth curved slightly. "Are you enjoying your courtship?"

"Is that what it is?"

"I admit I might not be very good at it. The rules are a little vague, but I gather it entails sending the one you care about gifts of flowers and candy, interspersed with episodes of dining and dancing. Under the present circumstances, dancing is out of the question."

"When I mentioned courtship, I wasn't implying that's what I expected from you."

"You've made it clear what you expect from me, and also that you didn't think you were going to get it. I decided to show you how wrong you were." His fingers tightened around the handgrips of his crutches. "I can't get down on one knee."

One more step and she would be able to touch him. "Why would you want to get down on one knee?" she asked, smiling.

The tension he had lived with the past several days began to ease. "I believe it's the custom when a man proposes."

"You don't want to get married again."

He nudged her with the tip of his crutch. "Let's sit down. This might take a while, and I'm not sure how long I'll be able to stay upright on these damn things. This is awkward enough without me falling on my face."

She helped him prop his foot up on the throw pillow she placed on the coffee table. Once he was settled, she took his crutches and leaned them against the end of the couch, amused at the role reversal.

She started to sit down on one of the chairs, but he stopped her. "No." He patted the cushion beside him. "Here."

The cushion gave only slightly when she sat down. She still wasn't close enough. He pulled her against his side, then slid his hand down her arm until he had a firm grip on her hand.

"I'm sorry I've been such a fool, green eyes. I've put us both through hell because I was afraid of failing again. Instead, I failed us both by not being willing to trust the future."

"Or me?"

He shook his head. "It wasn't you I didn't trust. I didn't trust my own ability to make you happy. Nothing had any meaning after I left your apartment. Marry me, green eyes. I need you, and I think you need me. I'm not afraid of marriage any longer. Just afraid of having to go on without you."

Since she was holding her breath, it wasn't easy for her to say "Why?"

Gazing down at her eyes, he could easily read the expression in them. He saw the love shining out and including him. He also saw doubt. She still wasn't sure of him.

"I don't want to go on without you, Meredith, because I love you. And before you bring up the fact that I might have been in love before since I've been married twice, I can only say I've never felt like this with any woman but you. For the first time in my life, I'm putting someone else ahead of everything else, because you are my life. In every way that's important, this will be my first marriage if you agree to be my wife."

Tears filled her eyes. The beauty of his words and his voice took her breath, yet gave her life.

She could only manage one word. "Yes."

It was his turn to exact more. Lifting her effort-lessly across his lap, he asked softly, "Yes, what?"

She wound her arms around his neck. "Yes, I love you. Yes, I want to live with you. Yes, I'll marry you."

His mouth came down hungrily on hers and the rest of the world faded away. The Rogue had found his home.

THE EDITOR'S CORNER

Those sultry June breezes will soon start to whisper through the trees, bringing with them the wonderful scents of summer. Imagine the unmistakable aroma of fresh-cut grass and the feeling of walking barefoot across a lush green lawn. Then look on your bookstore shelves for our striking jade-green LOVESWEPTs! The beautiful covers next month will put you right in the mood to welcome the summer season—and our authors will put you in the mood for romance.

Peggy Webb weaves her sensual magic once more in **UNTIL MORNING COMES,** LOVESWEPT #402. In this emotional story, Peggy captures the stark beauty of the Arizona desert and the fragile beauty of the love two very different people find together. In San Francisco he's known as Dr. Colter Gray, but in the land of his Apache ancestors, he's Gray Wolf. Reconciling the two aspects of his identity becomes a torment to Colter, but when he meets Jo Beth McGill, his life heads in a new direction. Jo Beth has brought her elderly parents along on her assignment to photograph the desert cacti. Concerned about her father's increasing senility, Jo Beth has vowed never to abandon her parents to the perils of old age. But when she meets Colter, she worries that she'll have to choose between them. When Colter appears on his stallion in the moonlight, ready to woo her with ancient Apache love rituals, Jo Beth trembles with excitement and gives herself up to the mysterious man in whose arms she finds her own security. This tender story deals with love on many levels and will leave you with a warm feeling in your heart.

In LOVESWEPT #403 by Linda Cajio, all it takes is **JUST ONE LOOK** for Remy St. Jacques to fall for the beguiling seductress Susan Kitteridge. Ordered to shadow the woman he believes to be a traitor, Remy comes to realize the lady who drives him to sweet obsession could not be what she seemed. Afraid of exposing those she loves to danger, Susan is caught up in the life of lies she'd live for so long. But she yearns to confess all to Remy the moment the bayou outlaw captures her lips with his. In her smooth, sophisticated style, Linda creates a winning love story you won't be able to put down. As an added treat, Linda brings back the lovable character of Lettice as her third and last granddaughter finds true happiness and love. Hint! Hint! This won't be the last you'll hear of Lettice, though. Stay tuned!

(continued)

With her debut book, **PERFECT MORNING,** published in April 1989, Marcia Evanick made quite a splash in the romance world. Next month Marcia returns to the LOVESWEPT lineup with **INDESCRIBABLY DELICIOUS,** LOVESWEPT #404. Marcia has a unique talent for blending the sensuality of a love story with the humorous trials and tribulations of single parenthood. When Dillon McKenzie follows a tantalizing scent to his neighbor's kitchen, he finds delicious temptation living next door! Elizabeth Lancaster is delighted that Dillon and his two sons have moved in; now her boy Aaron will have playmates. What she doesn't count on is becoming Dillon's playmate! He brings out all her hidden desires and makes her see there's so much more to life than just her son and the business she's built creating scrumptious cakes and candies. You'll be enthralled by these two genuine characters who must find a way to join their families as well as their dreams.

As promised, Tami Hoag returns with her second pot of pure gold in *The Rainbow Chasers* series, **KEEPING COMPANY,** LOVESWEPT #405. Alaina Montgomery just knew something would go wrong on her way to her friend Jayne's costume party dressed as a sexy comic-book princess. When her car konks out on a deserted stretch of road, she's more embarrassed by her costume than frightened of danger—until Dylan Harrison stops to help her. At first she believes he's an escaped lunatic, then he captivates her with his charm and incredible sex appeal—and Alaina actually learns to like him—even after he gets them arrested. A cool-headed realist, Alaina is unaccustomed to Dylan's carefree attitude toward life. So she surprises even herself when she accepts his silly proposal to "keep company" to curtail their matchmaking friends from interfering in their lives. Even more surprising is the way Dylan makes her feel, as if her mouth were made for long, slow kisses. Tami's flare for humor shines in this story of a reckless dreamer who teaches a lady lawyer to believe in magic.

In Judy Gill's **DESPERADO,** LOVESWEPT #406, hero Bruce Hagendorn carries the well-earned nickname of Stud. But there's much more to the former hockey star than his name implies—and he intends to convince his lovely neighbor, Mary Delaney, of that fact. After Mary saves him from a severe allergy attack that she had unintentionally caused, Bruce vows to coax his personal Florence Nightingale out to play. An intensely driven woman, Mary has set certain goals

(continued)

for herself that she's focused all her attention on attaining—doing so allows her to shut out the hurts from her past. But Bruce/Stud won't take no for an answer, and Mary finds herself caught under the spell of the most virile man she's ever met. She can't help wishing, though, that he'd tell her where he goes at night, what kind of business it is that he's so dedicated to. But Bruce knows once he tells Mary, he could lose her forever. This powerful story is sure to have an impact on the lives of many readers, as Judy deals with the ecstasy and the heartache true love can bring.

We're delighted as always to bring you another memorable romance from one of the ladies who's helped make LOVESWEPT so successful. Fayrene Preston's *SwanSea Place: DECEIT*, LOVESWEPT #407, is the *pièce de résistance* to a fabulous month of romantic reading awaiting you. Once again Fayrene transports you to Maine and the great estate of SwanSea Place, where Richard Zagen has come in search of Liana Marchall, the only woman he's ever loved. Richard has been haunted, tormented by memories of the legendary model he knows better as the heartless siren who'd left him to build her career in the arms of another. Liana knows only too well the desperate desire Richard is capable of making her feel. She's run once from the man who could give her astonishing pleasure and inflict shattering pain, but time has only deepened her hunger for him. Fayrene's characters create more elemental force than the waves crashing against the rocky coast. Let them sweep you up in their inferno of passion!

As always we invite you to write to us with your thoughts and comments. We hope your summer is off to a fabulous start!
Sincerely,

Susann Brailey

Susann Brailey
Editor
LOVESWEPT
Bantam Books
666 Fifth Avenue
New York, NY 10103

FAN OF THE MONTH

Ricki L. Ebbs

I guess I started reading the LOVESWEPT series as soon as it hit the market. I had been looking for a different kind of romance novel, one that had humor, adventure, a little danger, some offbeat characters, and, of course, true love and a happy ending. When I read my first LOVESWEPT, I stopped looking.

Fayrene Preston, Kay Hooper, Iris Johansen, Joan Elliott Pickart, Sandra Brown, and Deborah Smith are some of my favorite authors. I love Kay Hooper's wonderful sense of humor. For pure sensuality, Sandra Brown's books are unsurpassed. Though their writing styles are different, Iris Johansen, Joan Elliott Pickart, and Fayrene Preston write humorous, touching, and wonderfully sentimental stories. Deborah Smith's books have a unique blend of adventure and romance, and she keeps bringing back those characters I always wonder about at the end of the story. (I'm nosy about my friends' lives too.)

I'm single, with a terrific but demanding job as an administrative assistant. When I get the chance, I always pick up a mystery or romance novel. I have taken some kidding from my family and friends for my favorite reading. My brother says I should have been Sherlock Holmes or Scarlett O'Hara. I don't care what they say. I may be one of the last romantics, but I think the world looks a little better with a slightly romantic tint, and LOVESWEPTs certainly help to keep it rosy.

60 Minutes to a Better, More Beautiful You!

Now it's easier than ever to awaken your sensuality, stay slim forever—even make yourself irresistible. With Bantam's bestselling subliminal audio tapes, you're only 60 minutes away from a better, more beautiful you!

__ 45004-2	**Slim Forever**	$8.95
__ 45112-X	**Awaken Your Sensuality**	$7.95
__ 45035-2	**Stop Smoking Forever**	$8.95
__ 45130-8	**Develop Your Intuition**	$7.95
__ 45022-0	**Positively Change Your Life**	$8.95
__ 45154-5	**Get What You Want**	$7.95
__ 45041-7	**Stress Free Forever**	$8.95
__ 45106-5	**Get a Good Night's Sleep**	$7.95
__ 45094-8	**Improve Your Concentration**	$7.95
__ 45172-3	**Develop A Perfect Memory**	$8.95

Bantam Books, Dept. LT, 414 East Golf Road, Des Plaines, IL 60016

Please send me the items I have checked above. I am enclosing $_____ (please add $2.00 to cover postage and handling). Send check or money order, no cash or C.O.D.s please. (Tape offer good in USA only.)

Mr/Ms _____

Address _____

City/State_____ Zip_____

LT-5/90

Please allow four to six weeks for delivery.
Prices and availability subject to change without notice.

THE DELANEY DYNASTY

THE SHAMROCK TRINITY

- ☐ 21975 RAFE, THE MAVERICK
  by Kay Hooper $2.95
- ☐ 21976 YORK, THE RENEGADE
  by Iris Johansen $2.95
- ☐ 21977 BURKE, THE KINGPIN
  by Fayrene Preston $2.95

THE DELANEYS OF KILLAROO

- ☐ 21872 ADELAIDE, THE ENCHANTRESS
  by Kay Hooper $2.75
- ☐ 21873 MATILDA, THE ADVENTURESS
  by Iris Johansen $2.75
- ☐ 21874 SYDNEY, THE TEMPTRESS
  by Fayrene Preston $2.75

THE DELANEYS: *The Untamed Years*

- ☐ 21899 GOLDEN FLAMES *by Kay Hooper* $3.50
- ☐ 21898 WILD SILVER *by Iris Johansen* $3.50
- ☐ 21897 COPPER FIRE *by Fayrene Preston* $3.50

THE DELANEYS II

- ☐ 21978 SATIN ICE *by Iris Johansen* $3.50
- ☐ 21979 SILKEN THUNDER *by Fayrene Preston* $3.50
- ☐ 21980 VELVET LIGHTNING *by Kay Hooper* $3.50

Bantam Books, Dept. SW7, 414 East Golf Road, Des Plaines, IL 60016

Please send me the items I have checked above. I am enclosing $_____
(please add $2.00 to cover postage and handling). Send check or money
order, no cash or C.O.D.s please.

Mr/Ms _____

Address _____

City/State_____ Zip_____

SW7–4/90

Please allow four to six weeks for delivery.
Prices and availability subject to change without notice.